Braxton closed the space between them and lowered his head to hers. "It's never too late for something that's meant to be. Did you enjoy the song?"

"What do you think?"

"Oh, I think you did. It was plastered all over your lovely face, Sunshine."

Elle winced at the nickname he'd given her in high school because he said she brightened up his life. She used to love when he called her that, but now she simply loathed it.

She poked her finger into his hard chest while saying, "Don't call me that. You lost those privileges."

When he nestled his hand around her finger, the feel of his skin on hers sent a wave of shivers through her. She regretted being in his personal space, yet she couldn't move as he held her in a steady trance. He brought her hand to his lips and kissed it tenderly while studying her carefully.

"You are still the most beautiful woman I've ever laid my eyes on."

Her lids fluttered shut as he kissed her hand once more, and a long, relieved sigh released from her throat.

Dear Reader,

Elle Lauren is a resilient woman. The fact that Braxton Chase was a no-show on their wedding day made her stronger and made her realize that she could depend only on herself. She does miss him sometimes, especially when the orchids he sends after every fashion show arrive. Elle never stopped loving Braxton. Instead, she's learned to live without him. Now that he's back in her life, buried emotions have surfaced, and she wrestles with the notion of trusting him again.

Being an accomplished jazz pianist and living life in the limelight isn't all that Braxton thought it would be, especially without Elle to share in his success. He realizes his first love wasn't music after all and vows to make her his once more, but this time forever.

I hope you enjoy reading Elle and Braxton's second chance at their unforgettable love. Feel free to contact me at candaceshaw.net.

Always,

Candace Shaw

His
LOVING
Caress

CANDACE SHAW

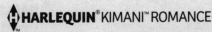

HARLEQUIN® KIMANI™ ROMANCE

Recycling programs
for this product may
not exist in your area.

ISBN-13: 978-0-373-86454-6

His Loving Caress

HARLEQUIN®

Printed in U.S.A.

™ www.Harlequin.com

Candace Shaw writes romance novels because she believes that happily-ever-after isn't found only in fairy tales. When she's not writing or researching information for a book, you can find Candace in her gardens, shopping, reading or learning how to cook a new dish.

She lives in Atlanta, Georgia, with her loving husband and their loyal dog, Ali. She is currently working on her next fun, flirty and sexy romance.

You can contact Candace on her website at candaceshaw.net, on Facebook at Facebook.com/authorcandaceshaw, or you can Tweet her at Twitter.com/candace_shaw.

Books by Candace Shaw

Harlequin Kimani Romance

Her Perfect Candidate
Journey to Seduction
The Sweetest Kiss
His Loving Caress

Visit the Author Profile page
at Harlequin.com for more titles.

Chapter 1

"Are you sure *he* isn't here?" Elle Lauren halted her steps on the sidewalk as tiny beads of perspiration formed on the back of her neck. "I mean...he does own the place." She ran her turquoise-manicured fingers through her thick back-length curls hoping to suppress any more nervous energy. Her heart stopped beating as she entered the revolving glass door into Braxton Chase's Jazz and Dinner Club, the hottest jazz club in Atlanta, which was owned by her ex-fiancé.

Megan Chase-Monroe bestowed a comforting smile as the ladies continued along the corridor to the mezzanine level. "Relax, Soror. My big brother is rarely here on Saturday mornings. It's his only day to sleep in and I promise you I didn't tell him you were coming."

Elle remained silent as she made her way up the grand black-marbled staircase and gripped the banister tight for fear of falling. She could barely concentrate as knots twisted at a rapid speed in her stomach. Her legs hardened with each step as if they were filled with lead. She suddenly felt as though she were walking the plank of a pirate's ship, and she realized she'd made a mistake. *He* may not have been there but his presence surrounded her and it began to restrict her breathing.

She hadn't planned on attending her sorority's scholarship fundraiser brunch once she learned of the location. However, Megan had promised that her brother would definitely not be present, and he wasn't even aware that she was in town that week on business. Still, she felt uneasy as she perused the massive club that screamed Braxton wherever her gaze landed. From oversized portraits of some of his favorite jazz musicians such as Miles Davis, Duke Ellington and Thelonious Monk covering the walls along with pictures of Braxton's band, to the black grand piano that sat center stage on the floor below. She'd tried to drag her eyes away, but it wasn't possible as her mind conjured up the image of his fingers caressing the keys just as he used to travel them along her body in the same tender, loving way.

Elle ran a hand down her bare arm to repress

the heated goose bumps that prickled her skin at the mere thought of being touched by him again. Luckily, Megan's cousin Tiffani Hollingsworth approached carrying three flutes of mimosas and handed one to Elle with a warm hug.

"I had a feeling you'd need this, Soror," Tiffani said, with a sweet yet solemn look on her angelic face. "Your expression is priceless but you look absolutely fabulous, love."

"Thank you. So do you, as always. You're definitely glowing with happiness."

Tiffani blushed. "I am. Broderick is a wonderful man," she answered, referring to her husband of four months. "But right now I'm concerned about you and your happiness. I know this can't be easy."

The ladies headed to an empty table and sat down. Elle set her untouched cocktail on the gold brocade tablecloth and slid into a chair. "I'm fine. Really. I know he's not here, but just the thought that I'm in his club is kind of nerve-racking." Plus, the fact that one of Braxton's jazz songs played in the background didn't help matters at all. She'd always loved the way he commanded the piano, and even though she hated him with every fiber of her being, she could never say he wasn't a master on the keys.

Megan reached across the table and patted Elle's hand. "Well, we're glad you came. We haven't seen you in ages. Now, I'm ready to eat. The chef here is absolutely wonderful. I purposely ate salads and fruit and drank water all week long so I can pig out today. I'm trying to get back to my prebaby weight, but with all of the events and cookouts I've been invited to this summer, that's easier said than done." Megan stood and smoothed down her flowing black dress.

Elle smiled. "You look fabulous, doll. No one can tell you just gave birth to twins two months ago."

"Thank you for sending me this beautiful ensemble." Megan twirled and Tiffani followed her action, wearing a short baby blue dress that showcased her long legs.

"Yes, me, too," Tiffani said as the ladies made their way to the buffet table where two chefs were cooking fresh omelets and waffles.

"You're welcome. They're both samples from a new collection I'm working on that will debut next spring. I love designing bridal couture, but I've decided to expand with dresses that can be worn to other wedding-related events. We're also working on another collection of everyday wear."

Tiffani placed strawberries on her plate while waiting on her omelet. "Well, I'm glad to be friends with a world-renowned fashion designer and will be honored to be a guinea pig whenever need be."

Laughing, Elle grabbed two strips of bacon and set them on her plate. "No problem, and as long as you keep sending me tasty treats from your bakery, you have a deal."

An hour into the brunch, Elle began to feel at ease

as she mingled and chatted with old friends. In the past ten years, she'd rarely traveled to Atlanta except to visit her parents. But once they retired from teaching five years ago, the Laurens moved to Destin, Florida, and bought a beautiful beach bungalow. The only reason for her visit to Atlanta now was to meet with an A-list celebrity who wanted Elle to personally design a one-of-a-kind wedding gown. Normally VIP clients met with her at her fashion headquarters in New York City, but the superstar singer was embarking on a mega tour for the summer and had rehearsals almost every day. Elle had designed evening gowns for the bride for awards shows and her client had always praised Elle Lauren Designs on the red carpet.

A loud screech in the sound system halted conversation and all eyes landed on the DJ booth. The guy mouthed out an apology before disappearing. Elle was somewhat grateful the music stopped because it was in the middle of a piano solo by Braxton. She'd never heard the song before but she knew his signature sound. She excused herself and turned to find Megan approaching her with an uneasy expression as she slid a cell phone from her ear.

"What's wrong?" Elle asked with concern. Megan was always bubbly and whimsical no matter the situation.

"Oh…um…nothing." Megan smiled and hooked

her arm with Elle's a little too tight. "I just hope the sound guy gets the music back on."

"Yeah, me, too." Elle stared at her puzzled. "I'm going to run to the ladies' room."

When Elle arrived, there was a quite a long line. Remembering there was a restroom on the bottom floor where she'd first entered the club, she jetted down the stairs to the empty restaurant area hoping no one else had the same idea. A movement out of the corner of her eye caught her attention. Turning her head slightly, her breath wedged in her throat and her pulse sped up at the hallucination in front of her. That's what it had to be, right? Braxton Chase couldn't possibly be standing less than a few feet away wearing a yummy smile across his handsome mahogany face.

Elle tried to move but her stilettos were deep-rooted to the floor. She racked her brain to find what she'd always said she would do if she ever saw *him* again. *Was it run the other way?* She sure hoped not, considering her skinny heels weren't made for such a feat. *Was it slap him?* Possibly but that would mean her hand would have to touch his smooth fresh-shaven face and then glide up to his shiny bald head. It definitely wasn't to kiss him. Even though heat puddled in her center as her eyes rested on his delicious lips that used to drive her insane. Her thoughts drifted further to his erotic tongue that had a mind of its own whenever it was on her body. *Was it to curse him out for not showing up at their wedding and humiliating her in front of their family and friends?* Probably, but she was too terrified at the moment to even open her mouth for fear of being tongue-tied. *That wasn't it, either.* Elle had promised herself that if she ever saw Braxton Chase again, she would remain composed. She could never let on to the fact that she hated but missed him at the same time. Though there was a part of her that wanted to run into his warm, comforting embrace and let the tears flow from having to spend the last ten years without him.

However, she didn't have a chance to carry out any of her thoughts, as the DJ appeared at the top of the staircase and shouted down. "Hey, B. Stop flirting with the lovely lady and bring the cord up here so we can get the music popping again."

Braxton jerked his eyes away from Elle for a moment. Taking a step back, she figured she could flee out of the revolving doors, jet down Peachtree Street to the parking garage, hide in her rental car and hopefully remember how to breathe again. Instead, Braxton tossed the cable up to his DJ and placed his focus on her once more. This time his stare was serious to the point it was almost sexy and commanding. The tension in her neck crept back again. She was supposed to be mad at him, not turned on, but he was the only man who had ever made her insides burn.

He hesitated for a moment before treading closer,

displaying a confident smile as if he were in control of the situation. "Hello, Elle."

His low, deep voice caressed her like satin on her skin as her name rolled off his tongue in a seductive manner. Braxton possessed a swagger he didn't have before, and it was downright intriguing. It reminded her of the summer before their junior year in high school when he'd returned from music camp. He'd shot up almost four inches during those two months of being away and had a faint mustache growing in. When he'd hugged her, she was overcome with nausea and panic, which was odd, because she'd always felt comfortable and secure in his embrace. That was the first time she'd realized she had a crush on her best friend, and then she ignored him for the next few weeks until he demanded to know what was wrong.

Now she felt like that high school girl standing in front of her crush all over again. Except this time there would be no hug even though her heart longed for one. And she hated that.

"Hi." Her voice was barely above a whisper, but she was relieved that the frog in her throat didn't make its presence known. "I didn't realize you were here."

"Normally I'm not. But I had something important to tend to." His eyes darkened, and he stepped toward her.

"Then I'll let you get back to it." She pivoted on

her heel and headed toward the staircase before the perspiration forming on her hairline appeared.

"Wait." He outstretched his hand as if he was going to wrap it around her forearm but quickly dropped it back to his side when she winced. "How long will you be in town?"

"Why?" Her tone was curt and abrupt as heat rushed to her face. If he thought she wanted to see him past this moment, he was dead wrong.

"So we can talk?" He closed the gap between them. "Maybe we can have dinner or something…"

The fresh scent of his woodsy cologne engulfed her senses making her forget for a moment her disdain for him. She gritted her teeth at his closeness and the fact that she had to restrain her body from nestling against his. Elle couldn't believe her thought process or her mixed emotions over the man who had left her. She silently chastised herself.

"We really don't have anything to discuss. I don't want to catch up on our lives, or reminisce about our wonderful memories, which clearly meant nothing to you. And I certainly don't want any explanations as to why you weren't man enough to face me on our wedding day. I know exactly why you didn't show up. I've known you since I was five years old. So unless you're going to tell me what an asshole you are, we don't having anything to talk about."

She stormed up the stairs before he could answer. Braxton was never one for a scene in public and wouldn't call or chase after her considering the music was still off and there were dozens of women upstairs. She made it back to her table and plopped into the chair next to Megan.

Elle let out a long sigh. "Your brother is here."

"Yeah…I just found out and I promise you I didn't tell him."

"Me, either," Tiffani chimed in. "Are you okay?"

"No. I'll probably leave soon."

Megan shook her head vigorously. "No. He can't know you're ruffled by his presence. You have to stay and appear unfazed."

"Yeah. I guess so." Elle shrugged and took a sip of her mimosa. "Besides, I left him downstairs."

Megan's face scrunched. "Mmm, no. Actually, he's talking to the DJ but looking right at you."

Elle turned her head slowly and right into Braxton's intent stare. A cocky grin raised up his left jaw along with a sexy wink. Even though it had been years, she knew him well. They'd been best friends since kindergarten before dating off and on in high school and all the way into graduate school. He was determined, confident and focused. He was also a stickler for a schedule. If Megan said he slept in on Saturdays, he did just that, which meant Braxton had purposely ventured to the club during the brunch in hopes of running into her. And he had, just as she was alone on the first floor. *But how did he…?*

Elle's eyes diverted to a security camera in the

corner above the buffet table and there was another one she'd spotted in the bar area earlier. Well, she had her answer but that still didn't explain how he knew she would be at the brunch. She believed what Megan and Tiffani had told her; they were aware of her disdain for him and would never betray her. And while she hadn't had a chance to speak to Megan's twin sister, Sydney, Elle didn't think she'd told him, either.

Glancing at Braxton again, she saw him fumbling with cords on a subwoofer. She let her eyes roam over him momentarily. She'd seen him grow from a scrawny little boy into a handsome, six-foot-four young gentleman and now that he was thirty-four years old, he was all man. Tight arm muscles bulged as he lifted a speaker from a cart and set it on the floor. She remembered him working out, but his muscles had never appeared so tempting before, and she could only imagine how his chest and abs looked under the black golf shirt. His warm brown skin was flawless and smooth all the way up to his bald head. She liked the bald look on him; it complemented his big soulful eyes and his confident smile.

Grateful when Braxton disappeared through a door in the DJ's booth, the tension in Elle's neck relaxed, and she hoped that would be the last she would see of him. However, for some reason, she had a feeling that wouldn't be the case. The fact that he was there wasn't coincidental and since he'd stated he wanted to talk to her, she knew he wasn't going to give up until it happened. After he was a no-show on their wedding day he tried numerous times to contact her, but her parents had prevented him from calling or seeing her. Over the years he'd sent white Phalaenopsis orchids—her favorite flowers—whenever she had a birthday, fashion show, or had won an award from the industry, and sometimes just because. There was never a note, but she assumed they were from Braxton because he knew of her love for the exotic plant and she had never revealed her favorite flower to any other boyfriend after him.

Just as she was starting to feel at ease again, Braxton reappeared. He pulled a keyboard to the ministage, then proceeded to hook the instrument up to a subwoofer. Her heart cringed. Hearing him on a CD or the radio rarely bothered her and if it did, she would simply turn it off and find something to do in order to suppress her hurt. However, this was different. She couldn't run out of the room. Especially considering she noticed a few of her sorors, including two who were hostesses in the wedding that never happened, glance her way with whispers. Instead, she placed a pleasant smile on her face and prayed that Braxton wouldn't dare play a song that held any special significance to them.

Braxton chuckled to himself as he glanced in Elle's direction. He could sense her discomfort, but he also knew she was a strong woman and under no circumstances was she going to let him see her sweat. That just wasn't in her nature.

When his sister Sydney had sent him a text message a few hours earlier that Elle would be at the brunch at his club, the wheels in his head had begun to churn. He needed to see her. He needed to apologize to her in person to clear his head of the guilt he'd felt for hurting her. Perhaps then he could finally be at peace with himself. Even though he'd tried on numerous occasions to see her after his no-show at their nuptials, her parents wouldn't let him in their home, had even threatened to call the police for trespassing. Eventually he'd learned from his sisters that Elle had moved to Paris, France, to continue her education in fashion design. When she returned to the United States two years later, he'd tried again. However, she sent a message through Megan to please stop all attempts to contact her; she'd moved on and didn't need him interrupting her life.

Braxton had respected Elle's wishes even though he did continue to send her favorite flowers on every occasion. He probably always would. But he never got over the guilt of breaking her heart. He understood not showing up would hurt her but at the time he was at a crossroad, and the one that held marriage wasn't the road he wanted to choose at that moment. They'd finished grad school a month before the day they were set to head down the aisle. It was all happening so fast, he barely had a moment to breathe. The pressures from both of their families to marry right after college suffocated him. It had been expected, and he thought surely he could go through with it. He'd loved Elle as his best friend and confidant since elementary school, and had fallen in love with her in high school. She was his soul mate and their connection had always been strong. However, whenever he wanted to discuss waiting a year or so, he couldn't bring himself to tell her. She seemed so happy to finally marry him. He chalked it up to having cold feet because he never, even for a moment, doubted that he loved her. Having attended different colleges, they'd been apart for six years, with the exception of breaks, because they'd agreed to complete their master's degrees before marriage. During that time they were off and on, dated other people, but never once did he doubt that she wasn't meant to be his wife.

Seeing her pictures online from her fashion shows and red carpet events always made his heart smile, but seeing her in person nearly knocked him off balance. Elle was breathtakingly stunning. He'd always thought she was adorable but now she was an elegantly refined, classy woman. Everything about her screamed exquisite and graceful, from her beautiful dark brown tresses with subtle blond highlights, to her lavender fitted dress that glorified her hips and butt in a way that made him very happy to be a man.

Even the way in which she spoke and her mannerisms were sophisticated and polished.

Her flawless brown sugar skin appeared edible and succulent, and it had taken everything in him not to grab her when she'd dashed up the stairs. He needed to feel her against him and kiss her delectable pink-painted mouth. He used to spend hours kissing, nibbling and biting on her lips and neck. If only to hear her soft purrs and cute giggles whenever his tongue would tickle against her ears or linger on the spot on the back of her neck that always sent shudders through her body.

Elle had been all his in heart, mind, body and soul. They'd been like one person for as long as he could remember, and he regretted the day he walked out of her life. However, now that she was in his jazz club, he needed to apologize. He knew in his heart she was still the only woman for him. When he'd learned she was in town he figured this would be his chance to ask for forgiveness in person. Seeing her now and the tiny sparkle in her warm chocolate eyes, made him realize that the unforgettable love they'd shared hadn't died. He vowed then to make her his once more, this time forever.

Chapter 2

Elle studied her flushed face and glistening eyes in the mirror of the ladies' room on the first floor. She wasn't even sure how she'd managed to walk down there. She had been in a daze and the heaviness had returned to her legs and her heart. Braxton had played their song and it had taken everything she had in her not to turn on the tears. For years she refused to listen to the song. But after awhile, hearing "Adore" by Prince had gotten easier. Until now. Braxton played it with so much emotion and vigor as if it was only them in the room. Once he was done, he'd given her the most endearing look, one that elicited heat to her center and caused a rage-filled shudder to travel down her spine.

Upon reaching the ladies' room she was flabbergasted to see the black wallpaper with orchids, solidifying the fact the flowers were definitely from him. In the plush ladies' lounge area hung oversized portraits of Billie Holiday, Ella Fitzgerald and Sarah Vaughn, who were some of Elle's favorite jazz and blues singers. Braxton had always been very detail oriented and even though Megan, who was an interior designer, had decorated the jazz club, it was his vision.

Exhaling to calm herself, Elle rustled through her purse to locate her keys so she could leave. The event was almost over, and she'd already given a sizable donation to the treasurer that would pay for at least two students to obtain their undergraduate degrees. She wasn't sure if she could make it back up the stairs to say goodbye to Megan and Tiffani, but she knew they would understand when she called them later. Glancing in the mirror one last time, Elle exited out of the restroom and straight into the sight of Braxton who was casually leaning on the opposite wall with his arms crossed over his commanding chest, next to a portrait of his jazz quartet.

Elle sashayed straight up to him as his eyes widened. She was sure he wasn't expecting her to do so. Her heels gave her a little height and confidence, because at five feet five inches, she'd always had to stand on her tippy-toes to reach him.

"What do you want?" she demanded through clenched teeth.

A sly grin reached his lips. "Is that a trick question? Never ask a man who finds you irresistible what he wants."

"Your compliments no longer work on me. I know you're not just standing here hanging out. You were obviously waiting for me. And how on earth did you know I was attending the brunch? Megan said you're rarely here on a Saturday morning, and I know neither she nor Tiffani would've told you."

"Syd sent me a text this morning. You know she always looks out for her big brother."

"Good ol' Syd," she said sarcastically. Elle hadn't had a chance to speak with Sydney, who, as a criminal profiler, was busy on an important case. But apparently she wasn't too busy to rat out Elle's whereabouts to Braxton. She wasn't surprised Syd told her brother. She had always been the main person dropping hints that Braxton wasn't over their relationship.

"She thought, perhaps, it was time for us to finally see each other. Finally face the music, and I agree."

"I don't need to *face* anything," she said angrily. "I'm not the one who left."

He nodded as if in agreement, with a solemn expression washing over his features. "I deserve that, and I know I messed up with you. Not a day goes by that I don't think about just how much I effed up."

"Yeah, you really did. I hope it was worth it, though. You got everything you wanted, right?" The question was laced with condescension as she stared straight into his eyes. "The platinum records, the awards, the accolades, the drop-dead gorgeous women and of course, the hottest jazz club in Atlanta. Am I missing anything?" Pursing her lips together, she folded her arms across her chest waiting for his reply.

"I don't have everything I want. I realize now more than ever what is missing, and why I've never felt fulfilled or truly happy about my success. I've missed you, Elle."

While he sounded sincere and she respected his honesty, he wasn't going to knock down her brick wall. He couldn't know that she felt the exact same way. She loved her career, but there was a piece of her that wasn't truly happy because he wasn't there to share in her success. However, she would never reveal that to him.

"Humph. It's too late for that."

Braxton closed the space between them and lowered his head to hers. "It's never too late for something that's meant to be. Did you enjoy the song?"

"What do you think?"

"Oh, I think you did. It was plastered all over your lovely face, Sunshine."

Elle winced at the nickname he'd given her in high school. He'd said she brightened up his life.

She used to love when he called her that, but now she simply loathed it.

She pointed her finger at his hard chest. "Don't call me that. You lost those privileges."

He then nestled his hand around her finger, and the feel of his skin on hers sent a wave of shivers through her body. She regretted being in his personal space yet she couldn't move as he held her in a steady trance. He brought her hand to his lips and kissed it tenderly while studying her carefully.

"You are still the most beautiful woman I've ever laid my eyes on."

Her lids fluttered shut as he kissed her hand once more and a long, relieved sigh released from her throat. Over the years, she'd dreamed of him placing tantalizing kisses on her body. They'd felt so real, as if he were actually there. But when she awoke, reality would sink in as she'd reach out to an empty pillow.

He rested his head on her forehead and took a deep breath. For a minute her pain was washed away and replaced with the strong bond they'd once shared. However, when his arms encircled her waist and drew her closer, her eyes shot open and she remembered this wasn't a dream. He was there, in the flesh, and she wanted nothing to do with him.

Snatching her body away, she took a few steps back and leaned on the opposite wall to compose herself. Being in his arms again, though brief, reminded her of the heart and soul connection they'd once shared. It was still there, and she needed to get away from him as soon as possible before the waterworks turned on and she gave in to his request to talk.

They stared at each other for a moment. Even though the music from the mezzanine level reached the lobby area, Elle could hear her heart hammer rapidly against her chest over the upbeat song. Before her was the man she used to love and trust. She'd shared her deepest thoughts, fears and dreams with him. Now she hated him. Though a part of her was actually overjoyed he was there. At one point in time he'd been her best friend, and she'd missed that more than anything.

Sighing, she broke their uneasy silence. "I need to go."

"I meant what I said earlier, Elle. I need to talk to you."

"We just finished talking. You admitted you effed up, you miss me, and I really don't care."

"You know what I mean."

"And I meant what *I* said earlier. We have nothing to discuss. You want to know how my life has been without you. Fabulous. Now I have to go check on a wedding gown for an auction. Goodbye, Braxton." She turned on her heel and hoped he didn't say anything else or follow her. She needed to jet to the car and fast before the tear in the corner of her eye rolled down her cheek.

"Oh, so you're attending your sorority's auction tonight, as well?" he asked in a pleasant, upbeat manner.

She cringed as she replayed his words. She really hoped he didn't mean "as well" as in he would be there, too. Pivoting toward him, she laughed nervously. "You're going?" she asked as calm as possible. Seeing Braxton twice in one day wasn't on today's schedule.

"Yep. I'm auctioning off an upright piano." Approaching her, he swept a tendril of her hair from beside her eye and tucked it behind her ear before running a finger down the side of her neck. "So I guess I'll see you tonight, Sunshine," he stated in an endearing tone that was accompanied by an arrogant smirk.

The mere touch of his finger on her neck was enough to send a raw shudder through her body that she managed to suppress until she rushed out of the revolving door, down the sidewalk and somehow to the safety of her rented BMW. Crashing her head onto the steering wheel, she exhaled and let the tears flow. Seeing Braxton without warning caused overwhelming emotions to surface that she'd hidden over the years in order to move on with her life. She'd missed him dearly and every blue moon she'd find herself teary-eyed from the pain that still lingered. However, she was irritated for letting him unravel her that easily. Braxton knew exactly which buttons to push, or in this case, which spots on her body to touch that would make her instantly let down her guard. He'd been her first love and the first man she'd ever been intimate with. She hated to admit that after all these years her body and mind were still under his control as if he'd purposely programmed it that way. The few boyfriends she'd had since Braxton never knew what the hell they were doing, and she usually ended up sexually frustrated because she never felt fulfilled afterward. She'd never craved or longed for any of them the way she did for Braxton. They'd always been in perfect harmony and in sync while making love.

Once Elle entered her penthouse suite at the Pinnacle Boutique Hotel in midtown, she found her assistant, Mya Collins, steaming the wedding gown for the auction. Elle had forgotten she'd given her a key and at the present moment preferred to be alone with her thoughts and a glass of wine. Tossing her purse on the foyer table, she mustered up a smile.

"I see the dress arrived." Elle walked over and eyed the princess gown carefully. She was a perfectionist and every intricate detail had to be on point. She ran her fingers along the crystals and pearls on the bodice that had been hand sewn in a basket weave design.

"Yes, Ms. Lauren. The delivery service dropped it off about an hour ago. It's absolutely beautiful."

"Thank you. It's one of my favorites. Did the other

dresses arrive as well?" Elle asked referring to a couple of evening gowns from her spring collection, one of which she would wear tonight.

"Yes, I steamed them and they're hanging in the closet. I love the black one with the side thigh slit. Very sexy. I know you had your heart set on wearing the pink ball gown, but I bet the black one would look hot on you. You have the perfect toned legs for it."

Elle tapped her chin. At first she wasn't even sure she wanted to go to the auction. Now that she knew Braxton was going to be in attendance she'd contemplated sending Mya. But she'd promised the president of her sorority earlier at the brunch she'd be there. However, that was before learning that what's-his-face would be present. Besides, the auction was just downstairs in the ballroom, which was why she'd chosen this particular hotel. She could make a quick appearance and jet back upstairs to avoid Braxton or she could stay for a while, completely ignore him, and agitate the hell out of him while wearing a sultry dress. And considering he'd always loved roaming his hands and tongue on her thighs, seeing what he hadn't had in a decade would drive him crazy.

"Mya, when you're done, help me try on the black dress to see what alterations I need to make. I think I want it cinched in more around the waist and stomach."

"You're going to turn heads in that dress. Maybe even find you a man."

Ever since Elle had ended her relationship for good with the investment banker she'd dated off and on for two years, her best friend and Mya had been relentlessly suggesting she find a man.

"Not exactly." Plopping down on the couch, she unbuckled her shoes and tossed them in front of her. "Just want to remind someone of what he could have had."

Mya turned the steamer off and joined her boss on the couch. "Wait a minute…you aren't talking about what's-his-name? The piano guy?" she inquired. "He was there after all?"

Elle laughed even though this situation was far from being funny. "Yep, you were right. He showed up."

"I told you he would be. He owns the place. Either someone apparently tipped him off that you'd be at the brunch or it's fate, and it's simply meant to be."

"Not fate. His sister Syd told him. I didn't have a chance to tell her not to do otherwise, even though I had hoped she wouldn't. He'll be at the auction tonight as well so I guess I would've run into him anyway. I haven't spoken to the man since our rehearsal dinner years ago, and now I'll have the pleasure of seeing him twice in one day," she said sarcastically, running her hand through her thick tresses. "Lucky me."

"You know your hair would look wonderful in

a swept up, tousled style along with your diamond choker and diamond hoops from Harry Winston. Showcase your regal neck."

"Mmm…that's a great idea. Just make sure the makeup artist you set up has makeup to cover up this." Elle lifted her hair up and turned her back to Mya. "Look at the fine print directly below my hairline." She ran her finger along the back of her neck.

"BC? You had his initials tattooed? That seems so out of character for you. Don't take this the wrong way Ms. Lauren, but you're so conservative and reserved."

"I was a freshman in college."

"Aww, you were in love," Mya said in a singsong voice.

"No. I was young, immature and head over heels in puppy love. That's all."

"And yet you still have it. You know you can have it lasered off, right?" Mya teased.

"Well, not before tonight. Just call her and also the hair stylist with the change of hairstyles. I'd told him I wanted it straight down my back."

"No problem. I'll call them now." Mya swiped her cell phone and iPad from the coffee table and retreated toward the bedroom door. However, she halted and turned around with an inquisitive expression. "Does he have one with your initials?"

"He had my first name intertwined with a treble clef over his heart. We got them together during spring break."

"I wonder if he still has it."

"I'm certainly not going to find out." Even though now she was slightly curious. However, he had numerous girlfriends over the years including one that seemed quite serious according to the tabloids. There was no way he'd kept it with all those women chasing after him. The only reason her boyfriends hadn't asked for the removal of hers was because she lied and said the initials meant "bold and confident."

"Bring all of the evening gowns and shoe choices out when you're done."

"Will do."

Resting her head on the back of the couch, Elle closed her eyes and let out a long sigh. Yes, she was fully aware she could have had the tattoo lasered off and had gone in twice to have it done. The first time she chickened out because she was told it would hurt and would take a couple of sessions for it to be fully removed. The second time, she was in one of her melancholy moods over Braxton and simply couldn't go through with it. It was one of the few reminders of him she had left, along with a CD he'd given her in college. Everything else was packed up in a chest at her parents' home, including her engagement ring that he'd refused to take back.

She rarely thought about covering the tattoo because she usually wore her hair down and very few people were aware she had it. If Braxton wasn't going to be in attendance at the auction, covering it with makeup wouldn't have crossed her mind because the diamond choker was more than likely wide enough. However, she didn't want to take any chances that Braxton would see it and assume she'd kept it because she still had feelings for him. But deep down she knew her reasons, even if she hated to admit them to herself. She'd never stopping loving him no matter how hard she'd tried, but she had been able to move on with her life without him. He rarely crossed her mind except the times when the orchids would arrive, and she'd withdraw for a day. But she'd bounce back every time and keep living. Now seeing him again had rustled up buried feelings. While she was curious as to what he needed to say, Elle feared the longings she had for him over the years would resurface, and she'd cave in to her desires just to feel his loving caress again.

Entering the ballroom, Braxton unbuttoned his Elle Lauren tuxedo coat and spotted his twin sisters waving to him from a table in the front of the room. He waved back and proceeded to search for Elle but there was no sign of her. The wedding dress she'd mentioned was on a mannequin on the stage along with his piano and other items for the auction. The cocktail hour had begun and there weren't many guests in attendance yet. He nodded and spoke to a few people he knew and then headed to the bar where he spotted his cousin Preston Chase wearing a wide grin as he typed something rapidly on his cell phone. Knowing him, it was one of his many female friends. Preston was one of Atlanta's most sought-after bachelors having made his millions from developing popular video games for cell phones, tablets and computers.

"What's up, man?" Braxton greeted. "I didn't know you were coming."

Preston tore his eyes away from the screen. "Hadn't planned on it. Tiffani asked me to donate something at the last minute. She's the chairperson over the scholarship fundraiser and has an astronomical goal in mind."

Nodding, Braxton read over the list of drinks that were being offered on a small easel on the bar. "You know your baby sister wants whatever event she is associated with to be a success."

"Of course. She's a Chase. We all have Grandmamma Chase's perfectionist trait in us."

The gentlemen ordered their drinks and strolled over to the stage to peruse the items for the auction. Braxton sipped his brandy while every now and then glancing back at the entrance to see if and when Elle would arrive. He hadn't stopped thinking about her since she'd reentered his life. During their years apart, when she crossed his mind, he could find something to do in order to distract himself. Now that he'd seen her beautiful face again in person, no matter what he tried, it was a waste of effort.

Braxton's eyes landed once more on the wedding gown. It was exquisite. He hated that he never saw Elle glide down the aisle in the gown she'd created and sewn herself for their wedding. He remembered her being thrilled and exhausted when she'd finally finished it along with five bridesmaids' dresses a week before their big day was supposed to happen. She'd been bubbly and overanxious for him to see her masterpiece because she'd designed it with him in mind.

He'd followed her career once she returned to the United States and began working for a famous fashion house in New York City until she took a chance and created her own line. She'd stated in a bridal magazine article that she loved designing wedding gowns because she wanted to be a part of a bride's happily-ever-after ever since her ex had been a no-show on her wedding day. Reading that part of the interview made him feel like a jerk. However, it had boosted her sales because every woman wanted a dress designed by the jilted designer.

The men continued browsing the items and Braxton came across a few things he considered bidding on. "So what did you donate?" He hadn't noticed Preston's name on any of the items.

A sly smile emerged across Preston's face. "A date with me." He stroked his goatee. "I figure they can start the bidding at around five. Heck, maybe even ten."

"Yeah, five bucks sounds about right," Braxton joked, patting his cousin on the back and then tilting his head toward some of the women who were around his mother's age. "I'm sure some of the golden-ager sorors would love to have a young cub."

"You're not funny, cuz, and I meant five thousand dollars."

"Well, good luck with that. What about Rhonda?"

Preston's face wrinkled with puzzlement. "Who?"

"The young lady you brought by the club last week who sat in your lap, fed you and nibbled on your ear all night."

"Nah, man. She's just one of my honeys in rotation. Nothing serious. Once I leave here, I'm jetting over to this chick's place for a late-night skinny dip in her pool. It was over eighty degrees today."

"Well, it is the middle of June in Hot Atlanta. It's only going to get hotter."

"I'm still beating you on the golf course this summer no matter what." Preston glanced at his watch. "I need this shindig to start so I can go." He downed his scotch and licked his tongue across his lips, slamming the empty glass on a nearby highboy. "Damn, on second thought, I may need to stay awhile longer. The honey dip that just strutted in is fine, and she's looking this way. I should just give her twenty-five thousand right now so she can bid on me. Oh, it's definitely going to be a hot summer." Rubbing his hands together, Preston tilted his head in her direction.

Braxton turned around to see who his cousin's next conquest was going to be only to discover Elle saunter into the room. And she was indeed fine as Preston had stated. The straight black dress encased her body as if it was created for only her to wear—which it probably was. Her windswept updo brought out her mesmerizing eyes, her swan-like neck and the diamond choker that was a reminder of how refined and classy she'd become. His gaze jerked to the slit that stopped midthigh that showcased her smooth, honey-coated legs. His thoughts travelled to the times when her legs were wrapped around his waist or entangled with his while they made love. Her legs, especially her thighs, had always been one of his favorite places to explore. *Did she purposely wear that dress?* Her eyes lingered on him for a second before turning to the hostess with a pleased smile as if she knew he was tempted. *Oh, yeah, she wore it for me.* And it worked as a strain against his pants emerged.

Preston tapped his chin. "You know she looks familiar. Do we know her?"

"That's Elle."

"Your ex? The one that you left at the altar, and we all thought you were crazy and just plain foolish?"

"Gee, thanks," Braxton said sarcastically as they headed to their table.

"Well, dang. She's definitely all grown up now. I

don't remember her being so…um…curvy and alluring. She's mighty fierce in that dress. I'm surprised someone hasn't wifed her up yet."

"Well, it won't be you so stop salivating over her." Even though Braxton was joking with his cousin, a tinge of jealously soared through his bones. The thought of her with someone else didn't sit well with him. However, he was surprised she wasn't married yet.

"Uh-huh. Don't worry, man. We're family. I remember Tiffani saying Elle may still have feelings for you. So what are you going to do about it?" Preston asked seriously. "There's some other men checking her out." He nodded toward a few of their colleagues who were eyeing Elle.

Braxton cracked a confident smile in her direction as he caught her eyes roam over him momentarily before diverting away as if she'd been caught. "I'm a Chase man. What do you think?"

Chapter 3

"Are you sure there's nowhere else for me to sit?" Elle asked the hostess for the fifth time. "It doesn't bother me to sit at one of the tables in the back."

"Nonsense, Ms. Lauren," the young lady answered, linking her arm with Elle's and escorting her toward the table where the Chase family was seated. "You're a VIP guest and you're auctioning off that beautiful gown. You have to sit up front."

Elle inwardly groaned but displayed a smile as she saw a camera flash her way. She could handle being in the same room with Braxton, but when she'd learned she'd be at the same table, it took everything in her not to bolt back to her suite. However, he'd spotted her as soon as she'd entered the ballroom so she couldn't escape. She had to remain composed and unbothered by his presence at least on the outside. On the inside her heart couldn't stop doing backward flips like an Olympic gymnast. He was devastatingly mouthwatering in his tuxedo and the way his gaze had raked over her like she was a succulent steak, was an indication that it would be a long evening.

She searched for an empty seat at the round table. Megan was seated next to her husband, United States Senator Steven Monroe. Tiffani, who was a newly-wed, was seated next to her husband, real estate mogul Broderick Hollingsworth, and Sydney was between her husband, power attorney Bryce Monroe, who was Steven's brother, and Megan. Preston and Braxton were still standing, conversing and glancing her way. She retracted her view from them and focused on the twins along with Tiffani who gave a reassuring smile.

There was an empty seat between Tiffani and Steven. If she could sit there that would be perfect. The other two empty chairs were next to each other. Braxton stood behind one, and she felt his heated glare burn through her dress to her skin. Elle was surprised she wasn't on fire from the way he stared her down.

"Hello, darling," Megan greeted, standing up to hug Elle. "You remember, my husband, Steven, from the fashion show last summer."

Steven stood, along with the others. She hugged

and acknowledged everyone except for Braxton who chatted briefly with a gentleman about the piano being auctioned off. She was relieved he hadn't been in line for a hug but as she was about to sit down she felt his presence behind her, pulling out the chair. The scent of his woodsy cologne filled her breathing passages, and she inhaled deeply. She'd always loved being surrounded by his scent.

"Thank you," she said politely, trying to avoid eye contact. She slid off her wrap and set it on the back of the pink tulle-covered chair before sitting. Braxton had always been a gentleman, going back to when they were in elementary school. He would open doors, stand when she entered a room and rarely let her pay for any of their outings once they'd started dating.

"My pleasure," he answered in a low, sensual tone that caressed a warmth over her skin.

His hand brushed her bare back as he pushed in her chair. She had to restrain herself from letting out a moan at his delicate touch that she sensed was done on purpose.

"You look radiant tonight," he whispered just loud enough for only her to hear.

She stumbled out a quiet "thank you." But held in the "you are absolutely scrumptious in your tux," because those were the words along with "damn" that had come to mind when she'd entered the room and his face was the first she'd encountered. Braxton was indeed handsome that evening, wearing a tuxedo from her mens' formal wear collection. He definitely could saunter the runway and send the crowd of women and fashion photographers in a frenzy over his smooth, bald head, provoking mahogany skin and muscular build. Not to mention his alluring smile that used to drive her wild when he would charmingly bestow it upon her just as he had when she'd arrived to the auction.

Braxton sat across from her and began chatting with the men about a recent golf outing. At first she was relieved he wasn't seated next to her but being directly in his view was worse. Even though he was egging Preston about fishing his ball out of the sand trap, Braxton continued to steal glances her way. She took a sip of her cool water to relieve the cotton that was forming on her tongue and the blaze that soared through her body.

Being with the Chase family again along with their spouses felt like a mini family reunion. Because she was an only child, Elle had been extremely close to the twins as well as Tiffani. Braxton's and Elle's mothers were best friends, having taught at the same elementary school for almost twenty years. She'd found it hard to be friends with the Chases after the wedding fiasco, but the girls were like sisters to her growing up and they had remained in contact. Her only request was that they not mention Braxton in any capacity, which they'd honored. But their silence hadn't kept her from being reminded of Braxton because a year after their breakup, his first jazz album had been released. It had been a major hit with three more CDs following within four years. He was pegged as the next great jazz pianist of the century and was all over the media. Trying to avoid knowing anything about him had flown out the window unless she stopped listening to jazz all together. But it was her favorite genre of music next to R&B and pop.

She was surprised, though, when he'd opened Braxton Chase's Jazz and Dinner Club about four years ago and appeared to place more focus on his business than his music career. It had been a dream of Braxton's, hence his master's degree in business. But the goal had been for him to open a chain of jazz clubs later in life. However, as he'd mentioned in a radio interview, he missed his family in Atlanta and wanted a break from touring all the time. Braxton still released CDs under his own label, all of which were platinum certified, and had won quite a few major awards, but for the most part he was out of the limelight.

"Elle?"

Megan's voice jerked Elle out of her thoughts. "Yes?" she asked as upbeat as possible, but unfortunately it came out in a loud manner. When she was nervous she spoke louder and faster. She decided to make a forced effort to remain calm especially when she caught Braxton's curious eyes on her, and took a sip of her water.

"I know you don't have a baby's line, but Steven and I would so love for you to design the christening dresses for Layla and Madelyn."

"I would be honored to design the twins' dresses," she answered, relieved that she sounded almost normal despite the fact that her stomach churned into a tight Boy Scout knot when Braxton had glimpsed her way. "When is their christening?"

"We're looking at the beginning of fall before Steven has to go back to Washington, DC."

"No problem. I'll be here until the end of the week working with a client, but I can definitely meet with you before leaving."

Elle noted Braxton raise an eyebrow though he continued his conversation with the men at the table. She cursed at herself for spilling how long she would be in Atlanta, and she knew he had made a mental memo of the information.

Megan's face brightened with delight. "That would be splendid, Elle. And you have to come by the house and meet the babies before you leave."

"I'd love to. The dresses will be my gift to you."

"Thanks, love! You're always so gracious and considerate. The onesies and outfits you sent for my baby shower were absolutely adorable. I can't wait to return the favor."

Elle simply laughed. She honestly didn't know

when and if that would happen. She caught Braxton's peculiar gaze on her when Megan mentioned returning the favor. While being married and having a family had always been on her list of goals, at age thirty-four, it no longer seemed to be as much of a priority as it had been when she was younger. She had girlfriends her age anxious to get married and constantly searching for Mr. Right, but after Braxton, her main focus was her career and building her fashion empire.

After dinner the auction started immediately, and she was grateful. The sooner she could leave, the better. Sitting across from Braxton's penetrating gaze was haunting and she was ready to say her goodbyes. However, Megan and Tiffani pulled her out onto the dance floor when their sorority's national party song came on and the ladies danced and stepped along with their other sorors to a cheering crowd. For a moment she had forgotten all about Braxton as she had fun dancing until she caught him staring at her from the side of the dance floor. After the sorority strut, she'd planned on slipping out once again, but the Electric Slide followed and that was her jam. When she glanced up to where Braxton had stood, he was no longer there. She breathed easy for what seemed to be a quick moment until she turned and noticed he was dancing at her side.

"Hi there," he teased with a wave. "I see you still love to dance."

"And I see you still can't." She couldn't help but rag him. Actually, he had danced quite well when they were younger, but he did seem a bit rusty.

"You never complained when we slow danced," he whispered. "I'm sure you remember being in my arms swaying to our song."

With a flushed face, she turned accordingly to the line dance, and he ended up behind her. Her heart froze, but she continued moving while hoping the song would hurry up and end. The floor was crowded and Braxton's chest was inches away from her back even though her gut told her he was too close on purpose. The dance floor may have been packed, but he was still too darn close. The song continued for a few more minutes but finally stopped when the DJ announced he was going to slow it down for everyone to catch their breaths and for the gentlemen to grab a pretty lady. Elle breathed easy again until she heard the first note of the song "I'll Make Love to You" by Boys to Men. It was one of their favorite songs, and she had a sneaky inkling he'd requested it. Either today was just one big cruel joke or she was starring in an episode of *The Twilight Zone*.

Elle's eyes immediately jerked toward Braxton to study his expression because nothing with him that day had been a coincidence or fate like Mya had suggested. She found him wearing a sheepish smile which suggested he knew exactly what he was doing. She turned on her heel to skedaddle back to their table, but he drew her effortlessly to him by the waist, her hands landing on the bend of his elbows.

Gasping, she eyed him sternly as her chest heaved up and down. She pulled away, but he held her firm in his embrace as a sly sneer formed across his handsome face.

He bent down and whispered in her ear as his tongue flicked over it. "Where are you going?" He raised an eyebrow and displayed a cocky grin as if there could only be one answer.

On the tip of her tongue she was ready to respond "nowhere, baby." In the past if she was in his arms and had tried to break their hug before he was ready, he'd always ask that same question. Her response would always be the same followed by a giggle or a playful kiss.

"Let go," she demanded through a clenched fake smile. "We are not about to do this."

"Elle, all eyes are on us right now and I know you're not one to cause a scene at your sorority's event."

Groaning, she backed up a step so she wouldn't be so closely pressed against him and slid her hands up to his shoulders. "Fine, one dance and then you have to promise to leave me alone forever."

"I can't promise that, at least not until we sit down and talk."

She closed her eyes and sighed. There wasn't anything he could say that would erase the pain he'd caused. But she knew how his conscience worked. He felt guilty. Now that he was aware she was in the same city until the end of the week, he would continue to try his best to see her. Luckily, he didn't know where she was staying unless of course Sydney had divulged that information as well.

She opened her eyes when he began to sing the words to the song, and she found herself completely against his body again. *When had that happened?* She hated to admit that the feel of him was comforting. The part of her that had longed for him and missed him was exactly where she longed to be. His warm embrace was even more defined. He was all man now. Gone was his lanky frame. He was strong and rugged. Irresistibly sexy and confident. He used to say that her body was the exact puzzle piece that fit with his, no matter the circumstance. Despite the fact that ten years had passed and both of their physiques had changed, she still fit perfectly, nestled in his arms. The thought made her breathing become unhinged. She needed room to breathe but she couldn't move.

The way his hands rested on her hips and moved her in tune with his body was a distraction. She wasn't supposed to enjoy this moment with him. She was supposed to be yelling and cursing him out. Instead, she couldn't remove her eyes from his handsome face as he continued to sing the song to her as if he meant every single word. It was torture and pleasure at the same time. The way her body was betraying her, she wouldn't be surprised if she completely gave in, because resisting him had never been easy. Braxton always had a way of looking at her with his dark seductive eyes that would make her weak. She decided to strike up conversation so he'd stop singing and gazing at her as if he was going to rip her dress off.

"I like your tuxedo," she said knowingly, running her hand down the lapel.

"Thank you. I wore it on the cover of my last album. In fact, all the cats in the band had an Elle Lauren tux."

"I know."

"You saw it?" His eyes sparkled and a wicked grin inched up his cheek. "You have my CDs?"

"Don't flatter yourself. Yes, I have your CDs and you have my tux."

"We were always supportive of each other. Maybe you can come to the club tomorrow evening. I'd love for you to see it when it's open and lively. Perhaps we can have dinner."

"You're pushing it, Mr. Chase."

"One dinner isn't gonna kill you, and we don't have to discuss the past if you're not ready to yet." He held up his right hand as if taking an oath. "Scout's honor."

"I'll think about it," she said, grateful the song was ending. In that short period of time he'd managed to crack part of her wall since she was possibly considering having dinner with him. She had to get far away from him before he bulldozed it all the way down.

"That's all I'm asking…for now. Thank you for the dance, Sunshine." Braxton seductively slid his hands over her curves and off her body. "Looks like we're still in rhythm. We always did dance like we were making love."

The image of such appeared at the forefront of her mind, and she had to shut it off and fast before she did the unthinkable. Suppressing a gulp, she conjured up a smirk. "Hmm…and your singing is still off-key."

He released a hearty laugh, but then closed the gap between them and rested a dark stare on her. "Baby, I don't sing. I play the piano and another instrument very, very well. And if memory serves me right, I used to make you go way off-key, though I'm sure you remember."

He glided a finger down her arm that induced a warm sensation to flow through her, and her nipples hardened as if cold air had hit them. Elle did remember all too well. She still dreamed of making love with him. He was the only man that knew just how she wanted to be caressed and handled. And he was right. The sounds and moans he used to provoke from her were totally out of tune, but she never cared and neither did he as his hands and tongue would travel over her body until she could barely remember her name.

"Yeah…well…vaguely. That was eons ago." She gave a cool shrug and strutted away with a purposeful slight swish until she made it back to their empty table. She looked out to see the rest of the Chase family on the dance floor. Preston had left immediately after the auction with his date who had won him for ten thousand dollars. She grabbed her purse from the chair and looked up to see Braxton standing over her with a heated gaze.

"Well, maybe you need to be reminded."

No need. I'm reminded in my dreams. She crossed her arms over her chest and eyed him carefully. "Maybe you should just give it up. That should come easy for you, right?" she asked sarcastically.

"I'm not that man anymore and you know in your heart this isn't over with. There's something still between us." He paused as a smug grin crawled up his jaw line and he leaned over, placing his lips just inches from hers. "I mean, you still have the tattoo on your neck."

Puzzled, she tilted her head up to him and stifled the swallow in her throat. "What are you talking about?" Elle tried to keep her tone calm and steady. She'd made sure before she left the suite that the makeup and diamond choker had concealed his initials. The choker hadn't been as wide as she'd thought but the foundation had blended well. Mya and the makeup artist had made sure of it.

"All the sweating you did while stepping with your sorors erased some of that makeup. I saw it when I was behind you during the Electric Slide. I'm flattered," he teased. "I'd thought surely you'd have it removed. That just gives me hope that you'll be mine again."

"You keep thinking that. Goodbye, Mr. Chase." She patted his cheek and walked away praying he wouldn't follow. She needed to get to her room and into an ice-cold shower. The evening hadn't gone as planned. She wasn't supposed to get hot and bothered over him. The goal was to irritate the heck out of him, not have him think she still wanted him and would even consider having dinner with him. And now that he was aware his initials still graced her neck, he was definitely feeling cocky and confident. But if he thought they were ever getting back together, he was sadly mistaken. Yes, she could admit that she still felt something for him. She knew in her heart that she would always love him, but she'd moved on and was happy with her life.

Elle made it into the elevator and was grateful she didn't see any sign of Braxton. Leaning against the wall, she held on to the rail as she took off her heels and watched as the doors closed. Being in the small space contained his scent which lingered on her skin. She breathed in deeply and out again relishing his manly fragrance. The cold shower couldn't happen yet because she wanted to reminisce about his scent intertwined with hers just a little while longer.

Once she made it to her penthouse suite, she tossed her shoes on the floor along with her purse and unzipped her dress as she headed to the bedroom. Being so close to Braxton had stirred up memories she'd suppressed, and he was fully aware, as her body had blatantly informed him on the dance floor. Plus, that dang tattoo still resided on her neck. *Didn't that makeup artist have waterproof foundation? Not using her anymore.*

Trotting to the bathroom, she flicked on the light and turned to see his blasted initials peeking through the makeup.

Smacking her lips, she undid the diamond choker and the earrings, carefully setting them in the box they'd arrived in. She'd rented them before leaving for Georgia and didn't want any mishaps with the flawless, expensive diamonds.

"Great. He probably thinks I'm still madly in love with him." Sarcastic laughter arose from her throat as she stared at her reflection in the mirror and began to take a couple of the pins out of her hair.

The knocking on the front door of the suite followed by the insistent ringing of the doorbell startled her. Zipping the dress back as best as possible, she stepped out to the front room. She hadn't ordered room service and Mya had a key, but she would've called first. Elle peaked out the peephole and saw Braxton standing on the other side of the door holding the wrap that matched her dress. In her haste to get away from him, she'd left it on the back of the chair.

"How did you know where I was staying?" she yelled out.

"I inquired after I saw you step into the elevator."

"Just leave it outside the door." She was too vulnerable at the moment to see him alone.

"No, someone could steal it."

"I'll take that chance."

"Elle, come on. Seriously. Please."

Against her better judgment, she opened the door halfway and peered out. She reached for the wrap, but Braxton grabbed her hand and pushed his way into the room. Kicking the door closed with his foot, he turned her back against it and mashed his body to her as his lips crashed over hers in a possessive, fiery kiss. The thought of saying *no* and *stop* had crossed her mind. But her lips and heart were screaming *yes* loud and clear as he sank deeper into her mouth, showing no mercy. Elle couldn't believe she was going against everything she said she wouldn't do with him. She had told herself that she wouldn't be in his arms again but that went out the window when they'd slow danced earlier, and she'd enjoyed every iota of it. She had also told herself that she wouldn't give him the time of day, but she'd opened the door anyway. Elle certainly never thought she'd allow him the privilege to kiss her again, but there he was with his lips on hers, kissing as if they hadn't seen each other in over a hundred years.

As she sighed against him, he let out a moan to match hers and his wicked tongue-dance sped up with every passing second. The idea of pushing him away was becoming hazy, and the fact that there was a part of her that was still mad at him only made her want to kiss him more. If just to remind him what he could've had all this time.

Elle ran her hands up to the top of his head and slid them down to his face. She was used to hair on his head, but she loved the smooth feel of his skin on her palms and continued running her hands over him as their kissing and moans intensified. His lips left hers, and trailed down her skin as he placed nibbles around her neck. A sound she didn't recognize as herself escaped her throat. She wasn't ready for his mouth to leave hers, but at the same time his hot tongue on her collarbone was exquisite. Holding on to her waist with one of his hands, he let the other one search in her hair and the next thing she knew hairpins that were strategically placed for her tousled updo were now being flung on the floor. However, she didn't care as Braxton's lips sought hers once more, but this time he delved slow and deep as soft whimpers sounded out between their lips. She held on to his shoulders to keep her balance.

Tears in the hollow of her eyes were ready to fall as her heart contracted in her chest. All of the pent-up desire for him was spilling out. She'd missed him with every fiber in her being. Her body trembled in his embrace as he continued to release passionate kisses on her mouth and neck. His hand grabbed one of her legs and yanked it around his trim waist. The tension of his penis pressed against her center throbbed hard through his pants just as it had while they'd danced. But on the dance floor she'd tried to block that acknowledgment. Now she couldn't. Her dress seemed to be easing down by itself and that's when she remembered she couldn't reach the zipper to zip it back up.

He slid his hands under the spaghetti straps and pulled them down until the dress fell below her breasts.

"Beautiful," he whispered, caressing one of her nipples gently before lowering his head and sucking on it.

He teased both back and forth as she held on to his head and moaned freely.

"I missed you, Elle. You hear me, baby? I've missed the hell out of you," he said in a gruff voice.

"I've missed you, too, Brax."

Braxton made her feel alive and wild all over again. Their intimate times hadn't been as frequent as they'd wanted because of being separated during their college years. But when they did make love, it was always special and each time had been new and different. The older they got the more intense and fervent their times together had become especially considering the long distance just made them yearn for each other even more.

Elle lifted his head and brought his lips back to hers as a guttural moan eased out of his throat. She always loved to hear him moan with pleasure. Even though he'd always said his mission was to please and satisfy her in every way possible, she wanted to do the same for him. The first few times they'd made love it had been all about her until she was comfortable and ready to explore other things. Once she was, she held nothing back and fully enjoyed hearing his lustful groans and making him tremble when he climaxed.

However, Elle knew none of that was going to happen tonight. She reminded herself that this was the same man who'd left her on their special day without a single word until sometime later when he'd realized his mistake. And even though she wanted nothing more than to rip off his tuxedo and make love with him in every position until the roosters crowed, it simply wasn't going to happen. Nevertheless, she was able to release a smidge of the pent-up desire she had acquired over the years for him. The rest of her evening would be spent in a cold shower. She'd have to spend not a night, but a year's time to make up for just how much her body had craved and yearned to be one with him again.

Abruptly she broke their passionate kiss, lowered her leg from around him and sidestepped away from the door. The confused expression on his face was priceless as she pulled her dress back up and grabbed the wrap from the floor and slid it around her shoulders.

"You should probably leave," she stated matter-of-factly, running her fingers through her loose curls as a few more hairpins slipped out.

He was obviously still in a daze as he ran his hand over his head in puzzlement. "Leave?" he asked in a bewildered fashion.

She gripped the doorknob and twisted it. "Yeah. You're good at that, you know. Shouldn't be too hard."

He chuckled at her sarcasm. "Elle, I know what you're doing."

"Then why are you still here?" She opened the door wide and stepped aside so he could exit.

However, he didn't leave. Instead he reached down to the floor for her purse, pulled out her cell phone and started typing something. He frowned for a moment then a naughty smirk appeared on his face.

"It has a passcode, Brax." She closed the door and stepped toward him.

"Yeah...well... I guessed the correct one on the second try." He shrugged and continued typing. "My birthday." An arrogant grin surfaced on his face. "Cool."

"Give me my phone." Snatching it out of his hand, she was curious as to what he'd done, but it was back to the home screen. "And it's not *your* birthday. It's the date I graduated from college."

"Still my birthday. I added my contact information so you can call me about dinner tomorrow night." He leaned down and kissed her gently on the side of the neck. "I'm not giving up this time, Sunshine."

After he left, she leaned her head back against the door while his last words rang in her head. She knew he meant them, and she had a notion that Braxton Chase was going to chase after her until she was his once again.

Chapter 4

Against all her reservations and the common sense that she *thought* she possessed, Elle agreed to have dinner with Braxton the next evening. He'd called her hotel room that afternoon to verify and for some reason she'd said *yes* out loud even though she was screaming *no* in her head. She'd wanted to call her best friend, Ciara, for advice, but she was on vacation with her husband at an off-the-grid resort in the rain forest.

As Elle entered the jazz club through the revolving doors, she glanced at her reflection hoping she'd made the right decision in coming as well as in choosing her dress selection. Mya had suggested something short and sexy. The hot pink bandage dress with the matching pumps fit the bill and her straight hair fell long down her back, completing the look.

"Hello, Ms. Lauren," a bright-eyed hostess greeted. "Mr. Chase is meeting with tonight's band on the mezzanine, but he asked me to show you to your table. Can I get you anything? Perhaps something from the bar?"

"A Vodka Cranberry with light ice, please." She glanced up and spotted Braxton leaning over the banister of the second floor as if he was waiting for her. Waving, he mouthed "five minutes" along with a "wow" as his eyes roamed over her body before he turned his attention back to the meeting.

She followed the hostess to the main floor, which was packed with patrons eating, laughing and dancing to the music flowing through the speakers. They walked up three steps that led to a huge all-white rounded booth that could probably hold fifteen people. When she sat down and scooted to the middle, Elle could see the stage in perfect view. As Braxton and the guest band approached it, his gaze met hers briefly before he grabbed the microphone to announce the quintet.

After the hostess left, Elle perused the menu, still in disbelief she'd agreed to dinner. But she wanted to see him again to prove to herself that she wasn't going to give in to temptation. At least that's what she kept telling herself, but a magnetic force was pulling hard against her heart. She'd tossed and turned all night remembering Braxton's lips and hands on her. Her body had responded naturally as it always had with him. He'd always made her feel like a woman but yesterday was different. They weren't teenagers or young adults anymore. The urges and passionate moans he provoked were new and exciting. It scared her and she was curious as to what else he could do now that he was all man. Tempting. Seductive. Delectable. Those were words that described him, and she crossed and uncrossed her legs at the thought of experiencing what he had to offer.

"Hello, beautiful."

Braxton's deep baritone voice startled her out of her amorous thoughts. She stared up at him. He was dressed in black slacks, a black button-down shirt with blue stripes and a blue vest topped off with a black fedora. She was almost disappointed he had on the hat but at least his bald head wouldn't be a distraction. However, he hadn't shaved and an alluring five o' clock shadow graced his face. She had to restrain herself from reaching her hand out to run her fingers down his cheek and to his juicy lips that had made hers swollen just the day before.

"Hey, Brax. This place *is* totally different at night. A very cool, sexy vibe."

"Thanks." He set his glass on the table and reached out his hand to her. "Can a brother have a hug?"

Sliding to the edge of the rounded booth, she stood and gave him a hug before settling back to the middle.

He sat on the end, and she was grateful he kept his distance. Braxton had always been respectful so perhaps he would keep his promise of not discussing the past. She wasn't ready for that. Heck she was barely ready to see him now, but they'd been best friends once and chatting and being in each other's space came easy.

"You're exquisite in that dress. Very sexy. Is it one of your designs?"

"No. It's a bandage dress by Lanvin."

Biting his bottom lip, Braxton raised a wicked eyebrow and leaned in slightly to her as his eyes rested on her cleavage. "So if I peel away the bandage it will reveal your supple honey-coated skin." He paused, as a seductive smize inched up his rugged jaw line. "Nice."

"Do you ever quit with the flirting?" she asked, trying to suppress the heat rushing to her cheeks.

"Can't help it when I'm around you, Sunshine."

"No flirting tonight, Mr. Chase. This is supposed to be a friendly dinner."

"Then you shouldn't have worn that dress."

She tried to hold a smile back but it was no use as one emerged along with tingles in her center. "I'll take that as compliment." She crossed her legs tight, hoping to ward off the warm sensation, but that action only made it worse. She had to get her mind off images of Braxton peeling her out of the dress. "This must be the best booth in the house. I can see practically everything from here," she said, changing the subject. If he said anything else remotely sexual, she'd demand that he close the oversized drapes that flanked the bottom of the staircase to continue what they'd started last night.

He opened a menu and then wrinkled his forehead as he set the menu back on the table. "Yep, this is my spot for that very reason. I can see the stage, the door to the kitchen and the dance floor. Whatever I can't see, I can look at on my cell phone using the security monitors."

She swished her lips to the side. "Humph. Is that how you knew I was alone on the first floor at the brunch? You were spying on me?"

"Nah…that was pure chance. I have to admit, though, I was watching you on the monitors in my office until the mishap with the speaker. We just both happened to be downstairs at the same time, and I have to say I was pleasantly surprised. Nervous though. My original plan was to stop by your table and say hi while I was up there. I called Megan to give her a heads-up, but fate had other plans."

"None of this is fate. Syd snitched and I doubt stopping by my table to say hi as if we were chummy buddies would've been warmly received."

"Yeah…well. I just needed to see you since you were going to be so close. Honestly, I wasn't sure if I was going to come out of my office or not. You looked happy, and I knew seeing me again could interrupt your life."

She laughed nervously. "It certainly did. Even though I wasn't totally surprised to see you. After all, you own the place. There was the possibility." She glanced back to the menu. "What should I order?"

"Everything is delicious. Our chefs can throw down in the kitchen. Are you still a picky eater?"

"Sort of, but living in Paris and visiting other foreign countries has expanded my palate." She read over the menu once more. "I think I'll try the Dizzy Gillespie Burger with cheese and bacon. No tomatoes. I haven't had a burger in a long while. My trainer is going to kill me when I get back to New York."

"You'll need to have it cut in half. Your dainty mouth is not going to fit around all that."

She noted a twinkle in his eye. Braxton had a habit of saying things with double meanings, and she had a notion his mind went straight to the gutter as did hers with his comment. Clearing her throat, she continued.

"With a name like that, probably not. So I'll have the burger well done and the Nat King Cole Slaw. Love these names." Giggling, she handed the menu to the waitress who'd returned and Braxton placed their orders. She wasn't surprised when he ordered the fried catfish and polenta.

She placed her focus on the band as they played "Prelude to a Kiss" but sensed Braxton's gaze on her.

She turned her head slightly to see him bobbing to the music but watching her.

"So Megan told me that you're thinking about opening up some more clubs?"

"Yeah, this one is doing quite well. When I changed the club's original name last year from Café Love Jones to Braxton Chase's, business boomed even more. My team and I feel now's the time to branch out. We're considering Memphis, Miami and possibly New York."

Her stomach fluttered when he said the last city. Not that it would matter too much. She knew he loved Atlanta, and it would always be his home, but she'd moved to New York to be far away from anything that had to do with him. It seemed she couldn't escape him no matter how hard she'd tried.

"I'm sure it will be just as successful as this one. Memphis would be a great location," she suggested. *Anyplace but New York.* "They have mostly blues clubs so jazz could be a nice addition. I go to the Memphis in May Festival sometimes and Beale Street is always crowded with tourists and locals."

"Mmm…yeah, but B.B. King's Blues Club is popular there as well as my cousin-in-law's dinner and blues club, so we'll see. Actually, a partner of mine is looking to reopen a club in New York and wants me to invest with him. It's in a happening location so I may check it out soon. I played there years ago when *My Sunshine* released, and I like the layout of the building. It's not as big as this club, and there's no second floor, but it's a cool spot. Just needs some renovating."

Elle simply nodded as he mentioned his first CD that was named after his nickname for her. The majority of the songs were inspired by her and were composed when they were still together. He'd called her his muse, and she'd sat for hours sketching dresses while he played and wrote music with her in mind. She'd loved those serene times together where they were both working on their craft while still spending time together. Every now and then she'd glance up and catch him staring at her. It always reassured her that they could both be successful in their careers and still make time for each other. So when he didn't show for the wedding, she was caught off guard.

She was glad when the waitress returned with her drink along with coconut shrimp and spinach dip with pita bread.

Taking a sip of her cocktail to calm her nerves, she found Braxton eyeing her with a tilted head.

"What?" she asked, reaching for a shrimp and dipping it into the pineapple salsa.

"What did you order to drink?"

"Vodka Cranberry. And I'm assuming that's rum and coke with just a splash of coke?" she inquired, remembering his favorite drink.

"Yeah, but when did you start drinking vodka? If

I remember correctly you like girlie, fruity drinks like wine coolers and Bahama Mamas."

"I'm a grown woman in case you didn't notice. I left those drinks in college."

"Yes, you are indeed grown. Grown and sexy, Sunshine, especially in that hot pink dress. I'm still trying to figure out where those dangerous curves came from. They're making me want to take a risk and speed along them, then slow down only to rev up again, very, very fast."

His deep, amorous tone made her want to experience all of that and more. Shifting in her seat, she took a sip of the drink hoping it would calm down the sensations that soared through her veins.

"Stop flirting, Brax." *Yes, please stop flirting before we relive last night but this time go further.* She pushed the drink to the side. *No more of that,* she scolded herself before it clouded her judgment. Instead, she grabbed a piece of toasted pita bread and plunged it into the spinach dip.

Braxton took a swig of his drink and leaned in closer to her. "I'll try not to, but have you looked in the mirror lately? You're one sophisticated and elegant woman. Not saying you weren't when we were together, but I grew up with you so I saw all stages. From a cute little girl to an awkward preteen to a blossoming high school student to an intelligent young lady in college. Sure I've seen more recent pictures of you in magazines and online but those photos didn't do you justice. You're a knockout. I'm not saying it to blow up your head or anything, but you're beautiful inside and out. Always have been." Pausing, he shook his head with a sarcastic scowl. "Damn, I messed up, huh?"

"Yes, you did, but we agreed not to discuss our relationship tonight."

"You're right," he said, with a slight grimace. "I'd hate for you to curse me out in my own club."

"I'm glad you realize you have that coming," she stated matter-of-factly. "Don't think for one second that just because I let you kiss me and I agreed to dinner tonight that I don't have disdain for you. You will feel my wrath soon enough." She smiled sweetly, swirling the ice around in her drink.

Nervous laughter arose from him. "Oh, I know. It's inevitable but I'm ready. So tell me what's on your plate while you're in town."

Dabbing her mouth with the napkin, she welcomed the subject change. "I'm meeting with a client for the next few days. She's getting married, and I'm designing her gown along with the bridal party's attire."

"Celebrity?"

"Yep, but I can't say who. Her engagement is a surprise until the September issue of *Beautiful Bride*. She'll be on the cover and in a spread in the magazine. All the dresses will be from my fall collection, of course."

"Of course. I have to say I'm very proud of you and your success. Your dresses are exquisite."

"Thank you. And I'm happy for your success as well."

The waitress dropped off their food and they ate in silence for awhile enjoying the band which was playing jazz versions of rap songs from the eighties. After a while, Elle noticed four young ladies being seated at a round table in the middle of the restaurant. One of them spotted Braxton, waved, and the other ones followed suit. Braxton inclined his head and raised his drink to them.

Her chest tensed at the exchange. She knew women lusted after him. Not only did they enjoy his smooth sounds on the keys, they also found him simply irresistible. It had never bothered her when she would attend his performances in high school and college. Other women had never been an issue to her knowledge. It was his music. Music had been his mistress, and Elle had never been able to compete with that.

"Do you know them?" she asked, taking a bite of her oversized burger which she ended up cutting into quarters.

He turned toward Elle and stuck his fork into the catfish. "Nope, just fans."

Stopping midway from biting into her burger again, she twisted her mouth to the side. "Those are not *fans,* Brax. Those are groupies. I work in the industry, too."

"Nah…you think?" He finished his drink and leaned back in the booth with a wide grin.

"The way they shot evil looks at me, they're definitely groupies. They came to the club tonight with a motive."

"Like you did in that dress last night or your dress tonight? If you're trying to drive me completely insane it's working, darling." He paused, lowering his voice. "Then again, you could've worn a potato sack, and I still would've wanted to get up under it."

Her skin flushed at the thought, but her wall *had* to stay up. "I have no motive tonight except to get through it."

"Ha! You forget I've known you since you were a thorn in my side at five years old."

"How was I a thorn?" She tossed her napkin on the table with a playful pout. "I resent that."

"There goes that cute pout you've had since that time, too. I think that's how I fell for you."

"Whatever. Our mother's were best friends and the twins were just toddlers when we all met for a play date. I had to play with someone," she teased. "Not my fault I could play checkers and Connect Four better than you."

"I was letting you win." He winked and took a sip of his drink.

"No, Maestro. You just couldn't play the…" She

stopped abruptly as she realized she'd called him by the nickname she gave him in middle school after he won a piano competition and a chance to play with the Atlanta Symphony at one of their shows. It flowed out naturally even though she hadn't consciously thought about that name in years. She silently chastised herself for the mistake. He remained silent except for the devilish expression that appeared when she'd said it. She had an inkling the wheels in his head were churning fast enough to make butter.

Despite the fact that she hated him for standing her up on their wedding day, there was still a part of her that was comfortable around him. She and Braxton were the type of friends that could go a decade without communication and pick up right where they left off. That irked her. She knew that was the reason she'd had no control over her emotions last night when she had allowed him to kiss her. And now here they were as if he hadn't left her. The thought made her dizzy for a moment. She'd always been in control of her life, but she couldn't control her emotions when it came to Braxton and she sensed he was highly aware of that.

"Do you want dessert?" he asked, whisking her out of her pondering. "The pastry chef here makes a slamming Turtle-pecan cheesecake. I read an interview you did with *Vogue* that you rarely eat sweets, but you'll eat cheesecake every blue moon."

Pushing her plate away from her, she leaned back

in the booth. "Oh, no. I'm stuffed. Perhaps I can take it to go. It sounds delicious."

"Of course. Whatever you want."

He called over the hostess who was nearby checking on tables and asked her to make a to-go box for four slices of the cheesecake.

Her attention diverted to the stage as the pianist performed a solo. He was good, she supposed. She'd found herself over the years comparing every pianist to Braxton. While some were noteworthy, none of them measured up to him. The man was the epitome of a musical genius. When he played, he was one with the music. The two were inseparable as he poured out his emotions and his heart through the melody. It always sent chills down her spine to hear him caress the keys. And while she'd admitted to him that she owned all of his CDs, she'd found it hard to listen to some of the songs.

She caught his eyes on her as he bobbed his head to the song. Finishing the polenta, he tossed his fork on the empty plate and pushed it to the edge of the table. He crossed his hands in front of him and continued his intent gaze at her. Fear swept over her as she noted the same passion from the other night rage in his eyes. She didn't even know why it had all of a sudden appeared. Their conversation had been friendly and safe, minus the part about her dress.

But she knew all of his facial expressions, mannerisms and moods. Pleasure rushed through her as he licked his bottom lip and scooted toward her until he was in the middle of the booth next to her. His hard, muscular thigh pressed against her almost bare one. Elle knew the dress was short when she'd slipped it on, but she'd been surprised at how much it rose when she'd sat down. Tugging on it hadn't worked when she had realized he was sliding over to her. The waitress stopped by, gathered their empty plates and quickly left.

Clearing her throat, Elle focused her attention on the band. "I wish you were playing tonight," she stated as she noticed his fingers tapping the table silently. She had to get the focus off them and since music was his first love, she figured they could discuss that and kill whatever sensual mood had arisen.

His forehead dented and his face frowned when he glanced at the band as if he'd forgotten where they were. His jaw clenched in a sexy smile as he turned his head to her. Resting his hand on her thigh, he gave a provocative squeeze and lowered his mouth to her ear. "Yeah, I wouldn't mind *playing* tonight. *All night.*"

Her breathing became restricted as his tongue gently grazed her ear. She managed to remain composed on the outside as people passed their table, some of whom waved or said hello to Braxton. Although he remained completely unaware of their greetings. Even when the waitress dropped off the cheesecake and asked if they needed anything else,

Braxton didn't flinch. She kept her eyes locked on the stage as his strong hand glided a tad higher under her dress.

"You remember how I used to play, Elle. Running my fingers and lips along every inch of your skin. Sometimes gently and sometimes…well…*not*. You would make those erotic purrs and I'd call you my little kitten. Hmm…you remember, baby? While I enjoyed last night's sample, I could barely sleep thinking about you. Wanting you. Needing to kiss your lips along with whatever else just to hear you and feel you tremble hard in my arms after you were completely satisfied. It took everything I had in me not to hop in my ride and speed back to your hotel to finish what we'd started."

Sliding her hand sensually on top of Braxton's, she turned her head to face him as her lips rested a mere inch from his. She gave a sultry stare as he parted her thighs and her mouth parted at the same exact instant.

"If you move your hand one more time, I'll break every single finger and you'll never play the piano the same again," she said though clenched teeth and a sweet smile.

Braxton stared in bewilderment at Elle's threat as he reluctantly removed his hand from between her supple thighs and placed it back on the table.

Chuckling, he scooted back to his original spot and rested his eyes on her.

"While your words aren't reflecting it, I know your body better than you, Sunshine, and last night proved there's something still lingering between us. I intend to act on it every chance I get. Even if I end up with a few broken fingers, my love, it will be worth it."

"What happened last night was simply left over attraction. So I hope you enjoyed yourself because it will *never* happen again."

"If you say so, but your flushed skin and the way your eyelids fluttered shut when I touched you say otherwise."

"Nope, your breath was just foul that's all." She shrugged, and followed with a wink and a cute giggle. "So glad you moved back over there."

He couldn't help but laugh. "That's my girl. I see you still have those witty comebacks, but it doesn't deflect the fact that you want me and I intend to make you mine again."

"You keep thinking that."

Grabbing her purse from the seat and her to-go bag from the table, she began to slide out of the booth. "I have an early morning appointment with my client."

Standing, he walked around to her side and helped her out. Squeezing her hand, he was surprised when she didn't drop it. "You're leaving so soon?"

"Yes. Besides, you have a club to run," she said, as they begin to walk out of the dining area. "And groupies to greet." She nodded toward a group of scantily clad women who were in the waiting area, all of whom smiled seductively at him.

"Nah…not my type. I'm more into the beautiful woman who's been swinging hands with me," he said in a teasing manner as they entered the revolving door together.

Her forehead wrinkled and she looked down as if she was shocked that they were holding hands. She snatched hers away as she stepped onto the sidewalk. He continued in the revolving door one more loop around as he laughed and then landed directly in front of her on the sidewalk. Sinking his hands into her waist, he drew her toward him and was surprised when she didn't pull away.

"It wasn't that funny, Brax. It's just a habit. We've been holding hands since we were children." She ran her fingers through her straight tresses. "No big deal. Just like last night. No big deal." She shrugged and began walking to the corner with him beside her.

"And yet you can't stop mentioning it."

Pushing the button on the walk sign, she turned toward him. "Think whatever you want. Anyway, thank you for dinner. I'm going to skedaddle to my car."

"Where did you park?"

"In the parking garage across the street."

"I'll walk you to your car."

"Not necessary. I parked on the lower level. I'll be fine. Good night, Braxton."

"It's almost ten o'clock in downtown Atlanta," he said as the digital sign changed to Walk. "You're not walking alone." He stayed a few steps behind, watching her long legs strut in the heels as her calf muscles flexed. Her bouncing butt was plump and tight causing a strain against his pants as he pondered whether or not she was wearing panties. Perhaps a sexy G-string thong because he didn't notice a panty line. "So do you drive much in New York?"

"Goodness, no. I have an apartment in Manhattan not far from my office, so I either walk or take a taxi. I hire a car service when I need to get to events around the city. I do own a car, but it stays at my home in Piscataway. That's the only place I drive."

"You remember when I taught you how to drive?"

She glanced at him out of the corner of her eye as she fished around in her purse. Pulling out a key, she aimed it toward a black BMW coupe to unlock the door.

"Is this a trick question?" she asked, as they stopped beside the car. "Some sexual innuendo?"

"Um…no. That's your mind in the gutter. I really was referring to the time when I taught you how to drive the summer before you took driver's ed, not the times when you were naked on top of me. But those were fun, memorable times, as well."

Groaning, she reached to open the door, but he beat her to it. "Now you know that's something you never have to do when I'm around."

Sliding into the car, she placed her belongings on the passenger seat and turned to stare up at him with a solemn expression. "Mmm…well you haven't been around, but I've managed just fine to take care of me." She said it quietly as a hurt expression washed over her lovely face that tugged at his heart.

Stooping down in front of her, he pushed a few wisps of her hair behind her ear. "And that's completely my fault. We still need to talk, Elle." He placed his hands on either side of her face and rested his forehead on hers. He was relieved when she didn't pull away despite the fact she sucked in her breath at his touch. "There are so many things I need to say to you…things I should've said then."

Placing a finger over his lips, she gripped one of his hands and stared at him empathetically. "Shh… not now. We just had a nice dinner, and I really don't want to be stressed out before meeting with my client. I need to save all my energy for dealing with her."

"I know you're busy this week but do you think perhaps we can meet again before you leave?"

Nodding, she pressed her lips together before letting out a long sigh. "I am busy, but I do want to hear what you have to say and there are things I need to tell you as well. This week will be hectic, but I'll call you. I promise."

"Thank you. I had a nice time tonight minus my fingers almost being broken. I'm glad you agreed to dinner."

"Well, a girl has to eat," she teased with a half-smile. "Now get up and close the door. You're not getting a kiss tonight."

Standing, he chuckled. "Not tonight, huh? But definitely some other time." He shut the door before she could slip in one of her smart-alecky remarks. He waved as she blew the horn.

As he headed back toward the club, he spotted Preston across the opposite street. He called out to him and his cousin sped up his pace.

"Hey man. You just got here?" Preston asked, checking his watch with a frown.

"No. I walked Elle to her car."

"Oh, snap, ya'll had the talk? You decided a public place would be better so she couldn't go off on you?"

Trekking through the revolving doors, Braxton waved to a few people who greeted him as they made their way into the crowd waiting to be seated. "No, just a friendly dinner. I need to go to my office to check the schedule. Are you coming or are you here to meet the chick of the week?"

"No date. I just left the children's hospital and decided to grab some dinner before heading home. So yeah, I don't mind following you to your office.

I'll watch the security monitors, and maybe I'll even have a date by the end of the evening," Preston proclaimed, smoothing his goatee.

Braxton laughed at his cousin's promiscuous ways. "Cool. You can order from there." Braxton stopped in front of a door with an Employees Only sign and entered his passcode. They proceeded down the hallway where all of the manager's offices were located.

Preston crashed on the couch when they arrived and grabbed a menu from the coffee table in front of him. Braxton strode to his desk and ran his hand over his computer's mouse to wake up his PC and sheet music from a song he was writing displayed on the screen. He moved the file to the back to pull up the schedule for the club.

"So how was dinner with the ex?"

"Better than I expected."

"That's good. Knocking down her wall, huh?"

"It's going to be a slow process, but I don't blame her. After all, I did leave her at the altar."

"Yeah, there is that." Preston tossed the menu on the table. He leaned back on the couch and focused his attention on the large flat-screen television with twelve split frames. "I don't know why I even look at the menu. I always order the same meal."

Braxton picked up the phone and dialed the hostess stand. "Hey, Nia. I need to place an order for Preston. His usual shepherd's pie with coconut shrimp and a cognac. Have it delivered to my table. We'll be there shortly." Hanging up, Braxton placed his focus on his cousin. "So how was the hospital visit today?"

"It was good overall. It breaks my heart to see those children suffering with cancer, but they're in good spirits, even when their hooked up to all those machines. I had a few of them testing out an upcoming video game I'm releasing soon. They enjoyed it and a percentage of the profits will be donated to the hospital."

"That's great, man. I love how you've been so dedicated in donating your time, not just your money."

"Thanks. I want to give back and I love when the children's faces light up with happiness despite everything they've been through. And considering I had leukemia as a child, I know what it's like to smile through the pain. I'm contemplating doing something this Christmas. Maybe like a big winter wonderland type thing for the kids."

"That's a great idea. How can I help?" Braxton asked while finalizing next week's schedule.

"Maybe you and your band could do some Christmas jazz songs."

"Done. Just tell me when and where and we'll be there."

"Thanks, cuz. So what's up with you and Elle? Do you think she's in the forgiving mood?"

"I think she's in a hot and cold mood. Last night

after you left the auction, we slow danced. Kind of flirted and moments later I found myself in her hotel room kissing her." Braxton released a sly smile as his thoughts trudged back to last night. Her lips on his and the sexy moans streaming from her mouth had kept him up daydreaming about going even further.

"Wait...what? Did y'all... Did you have the Preston Chase date pack? You know, the one with the Magnums, the getting-busy playlist with Al B. Sure and Brian McKnight, and the warming massage oil?"

"Nah, she pretty much kicked me out, but she did agree to dinner, which like I said, went well. I think the next time we meet it will be to discuss what happened. I'm ready. Nervous, but ready to face the music. She needs to know how truly sorry I am. I'm just glad she's at least speaking to me. I honestly wasn't sure what to expect when I first saw her after all this time. I thought she'd curse me out or slap me at the brunch, but she didn't."

"Elle needs closure. And I know women. If she let you kiss her she definitely still has feelings for you. They may be mixed at the moment...you know...like a love/hate situation but you two have a lot of history. It's not like she was just some girl you dated for a few years and then decided to marry. You were best friends since elementary school before hooking up. You two were inseparable and everyone knew it was just a matter of time before you dated. I remember our dads took us fishing for the weekend a few

weeks before our junior year. I think you'd just returned from music camp You told me that Elle had
been avoiding you all of a sudden. That she wouldn't
look at you and when she did, she'd blush. I was like
'dude, she likes you' and you were like 'nah, man.
That's my home girl.' The next thing I know she was
in the stands at the football games wearing your let-
terman jacket and rooting you on like you were the
star quarterback, not the drum major for the march-
ing band. I think you have a shot."

"Yeah, the mixed emotions were definitely present tonight. One minute she's all hot and bothered
and looking at me like she wanted to rip my clothes
off. The next minute, she pretty much told me I'll
never get the goods ever again."

"Yeah, I've had women tell me that. One big fat
lie. Heck, they're the main ones calling me at mid-
night talking all 'I'm horny. Whatcha going to do
about it?' Sometimes I go. Sometimes I don't."

"Yeah. I've been there, too, but I don't see Elle
doing anything like that."

"Well, when you have the talk, man up, and take
full blame because, well…you did leave the girl and
ruin her life. Just beg like Keith Sweat and Baby-
face combined."

Braxton pressed Send on the schedule to his general manager and closed the lid of his laptop. "Man,
you're a mess. Let's go. Your dinner should be ready

soon and there was a table of honeys in the dining area you may want to check out."

"I've been taking mental notes while talking to you. Looks like they're going to be in perfect view." Preston displayed a wide grin as they exited the office.

"Yeah, those are the ones. I think Elle got a little jealous when they waved at me."

Preston rubbed his goatee. "Mmm…interesting. You know after everything you've told me you may have a shot at getting her back."

"That's the plan, and this time I'm not letting her get away."

"Well, let the chasing begin."

Chapter 5

Elle leaned over the huge circular baby crib draped with a white-sheered canopy top and kissed the cheeks of the two little darlings inside who cooed and giggled as she continued gazing at them. "Oh, Megan, your daughters are absolutely breathtaking."

Megan beamed and picked one of them up and handed her to Elle. "Thank you. This is Layla."

"How can you tell them apart?" Elle asked, sitting down in one of the rocking chairs and cradling the two-month-old baby in her arms.

"Oh, a mother knows. However, one way to tell them apart is to look at their eyes. Layla's are more almond shaped like mine, and Madelyn's are more rounded and wide like her Auntie Sydney." Megan picked up the other baby and sat in the rocking chair opposite Elle's. "I'm so glad you were able to squeeze us in today. I absolutely adore the sketches Mya dropped off yesterday, and I love the idea of the dresses being different to suit their personalities."

"No problem. I wanted to see you and the babies before I leave. I'd meant to come over sooner but my client had me tied up for the last three days. She wants five dresses for the wedding weekend and that's not including the bridal party. But we got it all done so I'm headed back to New York tomorrow so my team can get started."

"I hate that you have to leave so soon. I only see you once every few years it seems, and you rushed off during the charity auction before I could say goodbye."

"Girl, you bolted toward the door," Tiffani teased, entering the room along with another lady Elle didn't know. "I saw you and Braxton having a good time."

Elle hated being reminded of that evening, but it was all she could think about the past few days as she contemplated calling him so they could finally have *the talk*. Considering their dinner went well overall, she was somewhat at ease with finally hearing him out. However, when he did call, she'd stare at his number on her cell and then toss the phone away from her.

"I was just being cordial." She decided against

telling them about the dinner date. *No, wait. That wasn't a date. Was it?*

"I'd hate to see what being friendly would look like. You two probably would've been arrested for lewd acts in public," Tiffani joked. "But I'll drop the subject for now. Elle, this is my friend Blythe Ventura. She's the artist of the painting you won at the auction."

Elle was grateful for the change of subject and even more elated to meet Blythe. "It is wonderful to meet you. That piece was so abstract and eccentric. I had to have it."

"Why, thank you. It was just something I was experimenting with."

"Well, it's going to look wonderful in my office. It's a very inspirational piece. Do you have a gallery here in Atlanta?"

"No. I own the Paint, Sip, Chat next door to Tiffani's bakery, but my loft is basically my studio."

The nanny entered the nursery to put the babies down for their afternoon nap and the ladies retreated to the veranda for lunch. Megan and Steven's chef had prepared an array of different foods to select from and Tiffani had brought a variety of cupcakes from her bakery, Sweet Treats. Elle was overwhelmed by the choices. It seemed she'd eaten nonstop since she'd landed in Atlanta. Usually she was busy with work and would only eat a salad or yogurt when she was on the go. She placed a little of everything on her plate and joined the ladies at the wrought-iron dining table.

"Megan, when are you going back to work?" Elle asked, hoping to keep the focus off her. She sensed the ladies wanted to discuss Braxton.

"We start taping the last season of *The Best Decorated Homes* in the fall. In the meantime I'm not taking on any major decorating projects. Steven and I just want to enjoy the girls."

"The last season? The Fabulous Living Channel cancelled your show?" Tiffani asked.

"No. Jade and I are going to do another type of show slated for next summer. It will still revolve around interior design, of course. We're the executive producers and creative directors, so we'll have total control."

Elle nodded, popping a miniquiche into in her mouth. "That's awesome. I know you hated not having full control of your show."

"Yes, but it was a great start and we're excited about the future."

Elle continued munching on her food in silence as the other ladies chatted. Her thoughts trekked to the other night in her hotel room with Braxton and the brief moment when his hand had rested on her thigh at dinner. The passion that had soared through her veins hadn't settled down yet and the pink orchid that had arrived the following day at her hotel room certainly didn't help at all. It was the first time the flowers were accompanied by a note, which stated "I miss you, Sunshine." She didn't even realize she was blushing and smiling until Mya had mentioned it. And she could barely concentrate when her client was relaying her vision of the gown. Even though Elle jotted down notes at the time, it seemed as if she was writing down gibberish and not real words. However, when it had dawned on her that she was in a business meeting and not pressed against Braxton, she jolted out of her daydream. Only then did she realize she had indeed written what the bride had said verbatim and managed to sketch out a couple of designs.

Braxton being back in her life without warning had knocked her off balance. She knew they needed to talk about what happened years ago and putting it off any longer was out of the question. She figured she could get it over with before leaving for New York so that when she returned, she could get on with her life again. This pit stop to the past had been nerve-racking and she couldn't concentrate on her job. No, it wasn't a job. It was her career and brand that she'd worked hard to achieve, turning Elle Lauren Designs into a multimillion-dollar, international corporation. Distractions were a nuisance and she needed to nip this in the bud quick so she could move on. The fact that Braxton wanted to win her back wasn't an option she was entertaining. Maybe they could be friends or at the very least check on each other every blue moon, but she couldn't let him back in completely. He'd broken her trust and her heart into a zillion pieces. While it had mended itself and was patched together with thread, she didn't know if it could sustain being hurt again by him.

Megan's whimsical voice brought Elle out of her deep thought process.

"My, my. You sure are in some kind of trance. Whatcha thinking about?"

"How I can't wait to begin sewing the christening gowns. I've decided to make them myself." While she wasn't lying about making the gowns for the twins, she wasn't exactly telling the truth about what she was pondering, either. And considering the look the ladies were giving her, apparently no one bought it, especially when Sydney strutted in.

"I may be late, but I know you're over there think-ing about my brother," Sydney said, setting her mo-torcycle helmet on the coffee table in the sitting area and joining the ladies at the table. "I got the ball roll-ing. Now it's up to the two of you to do something about it."

"Mmm-hmm. Not sure if I should be mad at you or not. I wasn't prepared to see him. You could've given me a heads-up, Syd."

Sydney shrugged, reaching for the pitcher of ice tea and filling a glass. "Yeah, but then you wouldn't have shown up."

"Are you finally going to hear him out?" Tiffani inquired. "Perhaps you both need the closure."

Elle exhaled. She knew the Chase women meant well and had been nothing but supportive over the years. "I've been contemplating that. For the most part I'm not as angry at him as I once was. Maybe now I can hear him out without wanting to throw him out the door like Uncle Phil used to do with Jazz on *The Fresh Prince of Bel Air.*"

Megan turned her chair toward Elle and grabbed her hands. "Sweety, over the years we've promised not to mention him to you, and we've respected your wishes. However, I will tell you that I know he's truly sorry for the hurt he caused, and I know he's still in love with you. He dates, sure, and the family has met a few other women but it's not the same as it was when he was with you. He doesn't speak about you, but I know when Tiffani, Syd and I all got married, he sort of thought you'd be there. He casually asked me who my bridesmaids were, which I thought was weird, but he was fishing for information. I don't want to say too much because he is my brother and I respect him as well, but I also know he messed up. We were all mad at him, but I know you were hurt. I'm not saying you have to forgive him, that's your call. Though, I'm sure there's a lot you need to get off your chest as well in order to have complete closure."

"I agree, Megan. And seeing him again has made

me realize that. I thought I had closure a long time ago."

"Well, I'm glad you have. Perhaps now you'll stop avoiding visiting Atlanta and we can see you more often. Just because you aren't with my big-headed brother anymore doesn't mean you aren't family. I hated you weren't in my wedding, and in Tiffani's wedding a few months ago on the Florida Keys. It was just beautiful with close family and friends only. You fall into that category. Hopefully, you'll be able to attend Layla and Madelyn's christening and not have to be concerned about seeing Braxton."

Elle nodded her head in understanding. "I'll try not to, and I've hated missing everyone's weddings and special moments. Perhaps Preston will be next in the Chase clan to marry."

Tiffani coughed on her slice of honey dew. "Girl, my brother is avoiding walking down the aisle like the black plague. I do wish he'd settle down, though. All these gold-digging women are just after him because of his money and pretty boy looks. I want him to find a good woman. Heck, I even thought about hooking Blythe up with Prez, but she groans every time I say his name."

Blythe dabbed her mouth and tossed her napkin onto her empty plate. "And I will continue to groan. Tiffani, you know you're my girl, but your brother is a player. I've dated those in the past and only ended up hurt and stressed. No, thank you."

"I'm just teasing, Blythe. He's an awesome big brother and uncle to Keith Jr., but his track record with women isn't. However, I hope one day he'll find the girl that will sweep him off his feet."

Elle zoned out again as the conversation veered toward Preston and his escapades. She knew it was now or never and though the latter was less frightening, she had to be a woman and get it over with.

An hour later, Elle bid the ladies goodbye and headed back to her hotel in midtown Atlanta. Upon arriving at her suite, her eyes landed on the white orchid on the coffee table, and she whipped her cell phone out of her purse and plopped on the couch. Her heartbeat sped up like a marathon runner about to cross the finish line while she scrolled through her contact list, found Braxton's name and pushed it.

"Hey, Braxton. Come on in." Elle stepped aside to allow him to enter.

"Hey," he said nervously as his chest tensed. Now that he was there to finally talk to her, he wasn't even sure where to begin. He'd already hurt her once and now he felt like he was going to do it all over again.

She looked young and innocent like she did in high school with a high ponytail, gold hoop earrings, fitted blue jeans and a white skinny T-shirt that enhanced her perky breasts. He gulped, thinking how was he going to get through this session when her cleavage was threatening to burst through the flimsy material. There would be time for that eventually. Right now he needed to jump over this hurdle, and pray she wouldn't push him out the door, vowing to never see him again.

"How was your golf game? Did you win?" she asked.

"Oh, yeah. It was a good day." *I just hope it's a good night.*

She motioned for him to sit on the couch, and she sat in the opposite oversized chair, curling her jean-clad legs under her. He studied her makeup-free face that held a look of anxiousness, and he wasn't surprised when she broke their silence.

"So...go ahead. I'm all ears."

Nodding, he glanced around the room and noticed for the first time her suitcases were by the door. She was leaving in the morning and he was glad she finally granted him the opportunity to talk. Clearing the frog from his throat, he exhaled and hoped their conversation wouldn't make matters even worse. However, he needed to tell her for his own peace of mind and closure.

"During the time we were preparing for the wedding, I felt like we were rushing into it. I know that's all we talked about in college, but when it was actually happening, I froze. I..." he stopped as the hurt rose in her delicate face and tugged at his heart.

"Let me finish the sentence for you. You punked out."

Tossing his newsboy cap on the table, he ran his hands over his head. "Yes, Elle, you are correct. The pressure from both our families, and the fact that I'd just signed a record deal, was weighing on me. You seemed happy about it, but you also wanted stability and I had doubts that I could be the man you needed me to be. You wanted a husband who would come home every day at the same time, have dinner and afterward cuddle, go to bed and start all over the next day. Before the record deal that was the plan. I'd gotten the offer to teach music at a high school here in Atlanta and you were interviewing for jobs in the fashion industry. However, all that changed. Despite what you may think, I wasn't trying to put my music career first, but at the same time I didn't want to disappoint you if I had a flop album and couldn't support us. I didn't want to drag you into that. All that was running through my mind leading up to the wedding."

Tearing her eyes away from him, Elle's face scrunched as she seemed to process what he'd relayed.

"So why didn't you discuss this with me beforehand?" she asked in a calm but firm manner. "Before you just left me like I meant nothing to you." This time her voice raised, and he noticed the fire in her eyes flame higher. He had a feeling that it wasn't going to be extinguished any time soon.

"I wanted to, but I chalked it up to having cold

feet and being scared about the future. You seemed so happy and I didn't want to hurt you, Sunshine."

"Oh, so you think being a no-show wouldn't hurt me?" she yelled, bouncing out of the chair and standing over him as her hands rested on her hips. "Braxton, I was embarrassed. Here I am getting ready to be your wife and you don't even bother to show up. I was terrified something had happened to you." Pausing, she closed her eyes as one of her hands rubbed over her heart momentarily. "I thought you were dead, because that would be the *only* reason you wouldn't show. Until Preston showed up and told me that you weren't coming and brought me the yellow roses and that sad excuse of a note that said 'I'm sorry.' That's all you had to say to me? You couldn't be man enough to face me? After everything I thought we meant to each other you had the audacity not to tell me face-to-face. And I waited for you. After everyone left the church, I waited for you. I refused to leave and I locked myself in the dressing room like a damn idiot because I just knew you would come to your senses or at least have the decency to tell me in person. I couldn't fathom why you would do that to me." Her voice cracked as the tears began to flow. "*Me*, Braxton. How could you hurt me, babe? What did I ever do to you for you to disrespect me like that? You had to know I was hurting. You would do that to me?"

She turned to walk away, but he stood and pulled

her to him as she squirmed in his arms. She was unable to break the embrace as he held her tight.

"Let go," she sobbed. "Please."

"No. What's our motto from our favorite Prince song?"

Sniffing, she looked up at him shaking her head as he wiped the tears off her cheeks. "No, it doesn't matter now. You ruined that."

Kissing her forehead tenderly, he lifted her chin so she could see the sincerity on his face. "It will always matter, Sunshine."

Sighing, she rested her head on his chest and wrapped her arms tighter around his waist. "That no matter what, we would always tell the other why we're hurting or upset even if the other person was the reason why." She wiped her face on his shirt and then frowned looking up at him. "It's hard to listen to 'If I Was Your Girlfriend.' For years I couldn't bring myself to play it. It was so us."

"Well at least you have a choice in the matter. It's a popular request so I have to play it while thinking of you the entire time and praying I don't tear up or something."

"I've cried a million tears over you."

"You're welcome to cry some more. I'll hold you as long as you need me to."

"I'm tired of crying."

"Elle… I am truly sorry for hurting you and not

being man enough to face you. I'm truly sorry, baby. I truly am."

Breaking away, she trekked to the other side of the room. "I know you are, Brax. I've known that for years, but what I can't understand is why you felt you couldn't come to me beforehand. We've been best friends since forever. We've always been able to talk about any- and everything. I've always had your back. I'd been nothing but loyal to you. What hurts the most isn't that you didn't show, it's that you didn't have enough trust and faith in me to listen to your reservations about getting married. You didn't think I'd understand? You thought it was better to not show up and have me look like a complete fool in front of our family and friends? If you'd communicated with me then perhaps we could've postponed the wedding for a year or two. Instead, you left me. I sacrificed a wonderful opportunity for you and you left me."

Puzzled, he came to stand in front of her and wiped the tears that had begun to stream again. "What opportunity are you referring to?"

"After you asked me to marry you, I was accepted into the Paris Design Institute but you wanted to get married a month after graduation. You said you wanted to start our lives together and couldn't wait any longer and I agreed. I loved you and for as long as I can remember I'd wanted to be Mrs. Braxton Chase. I knew you were shopping your demo around and meeting with record company executives. You are a musical genius, Braxton. Even though you accepted that job at the high school, I also knew that wasn't your true calling and you were simply doing that as a backup plan. I wasn't surprised when you received the offer. You're a master on the keys and a talented composer. Who wouldn't want you? I knew what I was in for with you. I've known all my life. Yes, I'd stated I wanted the stability like our parents but that was going to be impossible with you because of your career choice. But I was willing to make that sacrifice because I love you. I was overjoyed for you and your big opportunity. I was your number one fan. I was the cheerleader in your corner at all times."

"I had no idea that you'd been accepted during that time. I had assumed you applied after we didn't get married."

"You weren't supposed to know. I'd already said yes to you and then I received the acceptance letter in the mail soon after. Our mothers had already started planning the wedding and…I just decided not to worry about it. I wanted to be with you. And then you didn't even bother to show up."

Elle strode to the couch and plopped on it. Sitting next to her, Braxton grabbed her hand and was relieved when she didn't pull away. Instead, she gripped it tight as her leg began to shake.

"I guess we both weren't being totally honest with each other. You could've told me about the fashion school, but I still take full responsibility. I never meant to hurt you, babe. I hope you can find it in your heart to forgive me."

Turning toward him, she squeezed his hand again and answered softly as the tears welled in her eyes but didn't fall. "I'm not a grudge holder. I forgave you a long time ago."

"Thank you, Elle. That means a lot to me."

Closing her eyes, she exhaled and rested her head on the back of the couch. "I saw you not showing up as an opportunity to chase after my own dream. I refused to sit around and sulk over you. Not saying I didn't at all—that would be a lie. I cried more than I care to admit, but at the same time I needed a way to move on. Luckily, there was still space for me for the fall semester, so I hopped a plane to Paris, and I haven't looked back. *Humph*, maybe it was a blessing in disguise. We both have what we wanted career-wise and honestly there's a part of me that's glad we didn't get married. I don't think I would be the woman I am today if we had."

"Well, you are a sought-after wedding dress designer. If we'd gotten married your path may have been different."

"Yes, but I wasn't talking about my career. I was referring to being independent and relying on myself. I grew up real quick, Braxton. I think before all of that, I saw everything through rose-colored glasses. My life had been perfect and in my eyes was going to be even more perfect if I was Mrs. Braxton Chase. I wanted this fairy-tale romance with you. I wanted the house, with the white picket fence, two kids and a dog. But I had to learn to be on my own real quick because at one point, all my decisions were centered on us. I hated being without you, but I also enjoyed my new life without you. After fashion school, I moved to New York, started working for DaVinci Fashions and bought a house in Jersey. Just me, myself and I. I had a mortgage and bills. I was completely dependent on me and I loved it. Still do. I realized I didn't need you, or any man for that matter, to take care of me. So thank you, Braxton." She playfully punched him on the shoulder.

"You're welcome… I think."

"You know, sometimes, I chalk everything up to we simply weren't meant to be. It was just puppy love."

His heart clenched at her comment. Puppy love? What they had was far from puppy love. "Is that what you believe? Because I don't."

"No, but if you tell yourself something over and over you start to believe the lie. I loved you very much, Braxton. Have since the age of five."

"Do you think we can start over?"

"I'm not ready for that, Brax, but I do miss my best friend. You literally know me better than anyone. I've told you things that only you know. Even now if I need to confide or vent to someone, I don't.

I have my girlfriends and I do date, but it's not the same. So if we can perhaps work on being friends again that would be cool."

"So we're friends again? That kiss from the other night wasn't friendly."

"Don't push it. One step at a time."

"I understand, but I'm not giving up."

Elle laughed out loud. "I know. I'm looking forward to the chase."

Chapter 6

Elle sipped her coffee while perusing the samples from her design team as they all sat around the table in the conference area in her office at Elle Lauren Designs in the heart of New York City. They were in the process of creating a diffusion line for a popular upscale department store chain that wanted stylish clothes for the working woman at affordable prices. And while it was a big deal to her before she left for Atlanta, now she could barely concentrate on what her best friend and creative director, Ciara Matthews, was explaining.

"Do you agree, Elle?" she asked, resting her attention on her best friend.

After processing what Ciara had asked, Elle

sipped her coffee once more before answering. "Yes, I think adding purses, shoes and shades would be a great idea. We already have evening clutches and bridal shoes so I don't think it's farfetched. Get a research team together to see what styles are hot right now for purses but remember this line is sophisticated and elegant. The tailored look. Nothing too trendy. Think classic and timeless."

She glanced around the table as everyone jotted down notes while she tried to get her head back in the game. However, her thoughts kept trekking back to Braxton. For the past week, they'd stayed on the phone until almost three in the morning every night, talking about absolutely nothing just like they used to do. Unfortunately, she wasn't a teenager anymore and functioning off four hours of sleep was no longer tolerable. They were finding that their old groove mixed in with their present lives, and it was a wonderful combination. Luckily, he didn't mention anything about getting back together, and she appreciated that he respected her wishes to take it one step at time. Even if they never were a couple again, she was elated he was back in her life because she had missed him tremendously. Though, there was still a part of her that longed to be all his again if she could find it in her heart to trust him.

"Anything else?" she asked, roaming her eyes around the table at her staff shaking their heads and checking their cell phones. There were probably a million other things they needed to discuss but it was almost noon and the meeting had started at nine sharp. She may have been tired but Elle was a stickler for punctuality, even though she had wanted to cancel and lie in bed all day.

After everyone left except for Ciara and Mya, Elle retreated to the sitting area and curled up on the end of the couch next to Mya, who was adding pictures from a recent photo shoot to all of their social media sites.

"You sure are distracted today. Everything okay?" Ciara asked, strolling over and sitting on the opposite couch. "Perhaps you could use a vacation. I enjoyed every minute of mine."

"I'm fine. Really. I just have a lot on my plate. Besides, fashion week will be here before you know it and we need all hands on deck. It's crunch time and I'm still waiting on Kirk to handpick the models."

"He said it would be done by the end of next week."

"I hope so because the photo shoot has to be done soon. Just make sure he lands Leeza and Sophie. They're the top two supermodels, and I want them. Especially Leeza, since we're the reason she is where she is today."

Elle caught Ciara eyeing her with a peculiar expression and she had a feeling she knew what was really wrong. They'd been best friends since meeting and becoming roommates at the fashion college.

They'd hit it off instantly. She'd confided in her new friend about Braxton not showing up for the wedding and Ciara had been there through the occasional crying spells, the ranting and the orchid deliveries. She hadn't had a chance to tell Ciara what had happened with Braxton in Atlanta because Ciara had just returned from a two-week vacation to an off-the-grid resort. However, Elle had been itching to tell her everything, but she needed to do one other thing first.

"Mya, to your office and research some venues for a wedding dress pop-up store. I was checking the catalog and there are a few dresses on clearance that are discontinued. They're hogging space in the warehouse. About one hundred or so. We'll slash them lower because I want them gone before fashion week. Set up some appointments so we can visit some spaces. It needs to be big enough to accommodate a dressing room and sitting area. I think two weeks before fashion week will be fine. But it needs to be secured soon so we will have enough time to advertise."

"Yes, Ms. Lauren."

After Mya left with her instructions, Elle stretched her legs out on the couch. "Is it too early for wine?"

Ciara laughed. "It's almost lunchtime here but it's almost five in London." She stood, smoothed out her purple shift dress and walked toward the bar area. "You want white or red?"

"White in a red wineglass...practically filled to the rim."

Ciara's forehead dented as a frown emerged. "Okay, now I'm really starting to worry what the heck is wrong with you. Let me hurry up and pour so you can tell me what's eating at you. You barely said a word today and that's not like you."

"I saw *him* in Atlanta."

Ciara set the wineglasses on the table between the two couches and blinked her purple-colored eyelids several times. "Girl, I know you aren't talking about the name we never say. That piano guy?" She ran her fingers through her pixie cut and plopped on the couch staring at Elle in disbelief. "You went to your sorority's brunch at his club after you said you weren't going, didn't you? Dang it. I had an inkling he would be there despite Megan telling you otherwise. After all, she is his sister. She probably wants you two to make up and run through a meadow full of flowers barefoot. She's so darn bubbly on her television show I'm sure that's exactly what she wants."

"It wasn't her. It was the other sister, Syd."

"Told you one of them would."

"I know. I wanted to call you back, but I knew you wouldn't have any reception once you landed in the rain forest. But I decided to be a woman and face whatever came my way. Plus, Mya convinced me at the last minute to go."

"Fire her," Ciara joked, sipping on her wine. "I swear that girl needs to stay in her place."

"Ci Ci, you're crazy. But yes, he was at the brunch and the auction that night. We talked. We danced. We…" She couldn't get the word "kiss" out. She knew Ciara would have a fit.

"Well, did you at least curse him out for leaving you?"

"I did and it felt good to finally let it all out. I needed the closure that I've been avoiding and he did as well. He was truly sorry."

Ciara eyed her carefully with a glare. "And you believed him?"

"I do but I don't know if I can ever trust him again."

"Well, you don't have to. It's not like you're getting back together."

Elle took a sip of her wine. She didn't think she could utter the words that it was a possibility. "No, but we have decided to be friends again. Now that he's back in my life, I can't picture him not in it. We've been friends since kindergarten."

"Friends? After all that, you want to be friends? Girl, that man left you on your wedding day. He barely deserves your forgiveness, much less a friendship."

"Relax. He's in Atlanta and I'm here. It's not like I'll have to deal with him on a daily basis. I think it was more of a cordial no-hard-feelings kind of thing. It's not like I'm going to talk to him every day."

"Really?" Ciara kicked her shoes off and curled her feet under her. "And have you spoken to him since you've been back?"

"Um…a few times." She decided to leave off almost three times a day along with texting for the past week.

"And what about today? Your eyes were distracted by your cell phone during the meeting."

Elle shrugged and took another sip of her zinfandel. "He sent a text. That's all."

"He's trying to get you back, you know that, right?"

"I know," she replied quietly taking a sip of her wine.

"And you want him back."

"A part of me does and the other part is terrified."

Ciara smiled sympathetically. "I know. I shouldn't criticize you. I'm not in your stilettos. I just remember when I first met you, you were so sad and distraught. I felt sorry for you. You lost the man that you thought was the love of your life, but you bounced back and look at you now. You're one of the most sought-after wedding dress designers, and you've had a fabulous life without him. However, I've known you for ten years. Sure, you're happy career-wise. You've dated. You've had a few somewhat serious boyfriends that I know you cared about, but I don't remember you crying or giving a damn about any of them after the breakup. However, I've never seen your face light up the way it did when you mentioned Braxton a few moments ago. I know you still love him, and I know he hurt you. I'm not saying you should get back with him, but if being friends again helps you, then I'm all for it. Just take it one step at a time. Get to know him again. Both of you have grown and matured over the years. I've experienced your maturity firsthand because you were a naive thing who thought the world was all roses and orchids when we met. I think losing Braxton the way you did grew you up real fast. You're not naive and innocent anymore. You're a grown woman now. You know what your gut tells you. You'll know if Braxton is being sincere or honest. Just take it one day at a time, doll."

"Thank you for the advice, Ciara. I appreciate it. That's all I could think about during the meeting. Did I make the right decision by letting him back in my life? I feel as if I did and now I'm kind of excited to see how this next chapter will be. We've both matured, become successful in our chosen career paths, and we've admitted we still care for one another."

Standing, Ciara slid her feet back into her shoes and reached down for her wineglass. "I think you know what you're doing. You've always had great insight." She checked her watch. "I have a lunch meeting with Kirk to discuss the plans for the upcoming photo shoot but if you need me, you know I'm here. I'll always have your back."

"Thanks, girl. I know you do."

After Ciara left, Elle retreated to her desk and called Mya to run to the deli across the street to pick up lunch. In the meantime, she decided to work on the christening gown patterns for Megan's twins. Her cell phone ringing distracted her, but she was elated to see Braxton's handsome face on her screen.

"Hey," she answered in an upbeat manner.

"Hi there. Just wanted to check on you. I kept you up all night and not in the way I would've liked."

His deep voice in her ear sent a warm shiver through her body at the thought of spending all night with him in the way he wanted. But she had to be strong. They were taking it slow.

"I swear your mind stays in the gutter. I'm fine. A little sleepy, but after two cups of coffee I'm wired and running off adrenaline. And you? Did you get some rest?"

"I did. I slept well. I guess talking to you put me into a deep sleep, and again not in the manner I would've liked."

"Boy, quit. We're working on our friendship," she reminded, even though she needed the reminder as well. Yesterday at lunch a guy had asked her out, and she'd immediately answered that she had a boyfriend. She would've said no regardless because the man was way too old for her, but she shocked herself when she'd said with a confident and truthful tone that she had a boyfriend.

"I know. I know. So remember the jazz club I was telling you about in New York? My team and I are meeting with the owner of the building. If everything goes well, it will be mine."

"Oh, that's wonderful. So you're coming to New York?" Her pulse ramped up to one hundred in less than six seconds as she waited for his answer. She hated to admit that she wanted to see him, but she had begun to have withdrawals. Talking to him on the phone, FaceTiming and texting were cool, but she'd rather lace her hands with his and gaze into his enticing eyes while they talked or simply stared at each other.

"Yep. In a few days. My band and I are playing for the Fourth of July Jazz Festival at the Hamptons. In fact, I'm crashing at Megan and Steven's rental cottage. Would love for you to stay with me. Have you made plans for the Fourth of July?"

Stay with him? Running her hand through her hair, she stood and began to pace back and forth. "Oh…I see. Wow…um, no I don't have any plans, but I have so much work to prepare for an upcoming photo shoot and I'm overseeing some…"

"Making excuses? Scared you won't be able to keep your hands off me when you see me in my swim trunks?"

Probably, she thought. "Puleeze, dude. I can handle being around you. Even if you were in Speedos with a monster erection, it wouldn't bother me at all. So yeah I'll go to the Hamptons with you. No. Big. Deal." She plummeted on the couch, grabbed her wineglass and took a deep sip at the thought of his glorious, chocolate chest and his "monster erection." *Why the hell did I say that?*

"First of all, you'll never catch me in Speedos and second of all… I see you still remember what I have to offer," he said in a low, seductive tone.

"Don't flatter yourself. Besides, it will be you salivating over me in my bikini."

"You always did look hot in a two-piece."

"I still do, Maestro." *But now I'm going to do some extra stomach crunches and squats at the gym later today and lay off the carbs to be sure.*

He released a hearty laugh. "I bet you do. I gotta run. Rehearsing for the mayor's ball tonight but I'll call you later with the details."

"Sounds good."

After Elle hung up with Braxton, Mya entered with bags from the deli. Her nose wrinkled when she saw Elle sipping wine but she didn't say anything. Instead, she began opening the bags and setting the containers on the coffee table in front of Elle.

"I got your favorite chicken salad on a croissant and a small Caesar salad. Oh, and there's a yogurt with granola, as well. I brought you peach tea but it seems you already have something to drink…" Mya glanced at the wineglass.

"Okay, so I normally don't drink alcohol in the middle of the workday, but Ciara and I needed to have a conversation and wine just went well with it."

"No problem. I'm going to go back to my office, eat and continue working on the pop-up store project. Do you need anything else?"

"No…just be ready at three for the warehouse walk-through. Oh, wait. Check to see if any of my fashion designer friends have some hot bikinis and sarongs. I'm going to the Hamptons for the Fourth of July and need some new ones."

Mya tapped her chin with smirk. "The Hamptons? For the Fourth of July? Mmm-hmm."

"Um…yeah. So? I go to the Hamptons every summer."

"Yes, but I recently saw the flier for the jazz festival and a certain quartet is on there. The Braxton Chase Quartet. Interesting."

After opening the salad container, Elle picked a crouton off the top and popped it in her mouth. "Yes, he invited me to hang with him for a few days in the Hamptons. No big deal." Elle shrugged and mixed the salad around. *And it wasn't a big deal. We're friends, and I have willpower.*

"How many *hot* bikinis do you want? Should I add anything else to the list? Lingerie? A Brazilian wax?" Mya teased, walking toward the door. "Toodles."

Elle called out in a joking manner, "You know, Ciara suggested I fire you for making me go to the brunch in the first place."

"Yeah, yeah. Ciara says you should fire me all the time. Just make sure I get an invite to the wedding," Mya said, closing the door behind her.

Wedding? Getting married was no longer on her goal list.

She'd had proposals from two boyfriends and while she did care for them, she couldn't see herself married to either one. Ciara and their other friends suggested she was scared of the actual wedding ceremony and feared being jilted again but that wasn't the case. There simply wasn't any chemistry. She didn't love them as she had Braxton. Heck, she didn't even know them like that. Sure, she knew the basic, generic things but the deep conversations and the knowing what they were thinking just by facial expressions wasn't present. She'd tried hard as she could to love Connor Prescott, the investment banker. Her parents adored him and his family adored her, but there was just something missing that she could never pinpoint. Perhaps it was that his snoring, chewing and lame jokes bothered her to no end. Braxton's snoring had never bothered her. Even when she would be away from New York for a week or more at a time, she didn't miss Connor at all. And that was all the proof she needed to know that he simply wasn't the one.

Taking a bite of her salad, Elle's thoughts trekked back to Mya's words. At this point, Elle wasn't sure about getting back with him much less marrying the man. Even though the sad truth was that she couldn't see herself married to anyone but Braxton.

Chapter 7

"This is absolutely exquisite," Elle stated as she walked into the tiled foyer of the Cape Cod cottage on the Hamptons. She could see through to the over-sized great room with plush off-white couches with matching comfy, huge chairs topped with gold and dark blue toss pillows. In the middle of the room was a white baby grand piano set in front of an enormous picture window that overlooked the inviting blue ocean.

"Thank you. Glad you like it." Braxton replied as they walked through to the great room. To the right was an open gourmet kitchen with off-white antique cabinets, stainless steel appliances and beige granite countertops. A round glass table with black wrought-iron chairs sat in the breakfast nook amidst bay windows and puffy burgundy valances that matched placemats and napkins on the beautifully set table. Everything was decorated with perfection and she wasn't surprised.

"This place has Megan written all over it."

"Yep. Baby sis is very talented." Braxton sat on the piano bench and Elle joined him.

His scent hit her nose and she almost regretted sitting so close. She was tempted to straddle his lap but her key word for the weekend was willpower. And considering he looked absolutely scrumptious in a pair of khaki shorts and a red golf shirt that wasn't hiding his toned mocha arms, she needed all the willpower she could muster up.

"She decorated my second home in New Jersey a few summers ago. It's absolutely gorgeous. I'm sometimes scared to touch anything because I don't want to mess it up."

"I didn't know she decorated your home."

Elle ran her fingers along the keys of the piano. "You weren't supposed to."

"Well, I have to admit whenever I asked my sisters about you they didn't answer. Syd would say 'Let the internet be your friend' in a sarcastic way."

Elle laughed. "That sounds just like her."

"Do you remember how to play?"

"Uh…no." She wrinkled her nose as her brow creased. She loved music thanks to him, but she had no musical ability whatsoever. "I do believe you taught me how to play three songs, though. The only one I remember is "Mary Had a Little Lamb" and that's with one finger, not ten. My lessons usually ended unfinished, as I'd find myself straddling my piano teacher and kissing him as my back would play the keys better than I ever could."

Nodding his head, he winked at her with an intoxicating grin. "Those were some good times. You were my favorite student. Let me see what you remember."

"You can't be serious, Maestro."

"It's all in fun."

Groaning, she started to play with one finger, or rather bang the keys with one finger, painstakingly skipping over and playing the wrong notes. It was embarrassing to mess up in front of him. Sure he was her homeboy, but he was also a musical genius, a master at his craft. She hated that she'd even attempted to play something so simple and still effed it up.

Braxton covered his ears and Elle playfully pinched him on the arm.

"Sunshine. Stop. Just stop," he teased, taking her hands and holding them tight in his lap.

"I glad you're finding this amusing. I told you I don't remember. Besides, that's not where my talents or creativity lie."

A sinful grin rose up the corner of his mouth as

he leaned over and placed a seductive kiss to the side of her neck, eliciting a surprised yet pleased gasp from her. She pushed away from him to the edge of the bench before she showed him just how talented she was.

"Down, boy. I was referring to my designs, not… kissing and stuff."

"And stuff? Mmm… I remember that quite well. But seriously, you're the best in your field, Sunshine. I've always known that. I especially love that black dress from the auction. It had all your ample curves on display. You wouldn't happen to have one in every color? The girls were looking mighty ripe and delicious that night." He played a few notes from "My, My, My" by Johnny Gill. "Glad I got a little sample."

Smacking her lips, she shook her head. "You never quit. Don't make me play another selection."

"No, no." He waved his hands in front of him laughing. "How about I play and you take a tour of the house and relax. Any requests?" He raised his eyebrow with a knowing expression as if he already knew what she wanted to hear.

Elle had plenty of requests, but decided she wasn't ready to hear any of the songs he'd written for her. It was too soon and a few still made her teary-eyed. "How about you practice your set for the jazz fest tomorrow."

"I've been at rehearsal all day with the band."

Rising, she retreated to the window to stare out

at the beautiful shades of the sky as the sun began to set, giving her an idea for pastel, tranquil summer bridesmaids' dresses.

"Then rest your hands. I'm going to go outside and take pictures of the sky. It's very inspiring."

"Cool. I'll take your bags to your room. You have the master suite. It's on the other side of the kitchen."

Elle was glad he'd answered the question that had brewed in her mind all day. She'd wondered about their sleeping arrangements. Since it was also a rental, she'd looked up the information for the home that morning and saw that it had four bedrooms. "And where are you sleeping, Mr. Chase?"

"Calm down. In the in-law suite on the other side. It's basically the same as the master unless you'd prefer me to sleep with you." His lips rose slyly up his jaw.

"No."

"Very well. We could've had a slumber party."

"Aren't we too old for slumber parties?"

"We can stay up and catch up," he suggested.

"That's sounds like a plan, but out here, not in the bedroom. What's the plan for dinner?"

"The chef will be here soon."

"Chef?"

"Yes, I hired one to cook dinner. I hope you like lobster."

"I love it."

"Perfect. Would you like to eat out on the veranda? It's enclosed, so no bugs."

"That would be lovely. Thank you." She exited through the French doors leading outside and before she could close them she heard the prelude of the first song he'd ever written for her and kept the door slightly ajar. Of all the songs, she thought. That was the one that bothered her the most. He'd written it while she'd slept after their first time making love. She'd woken up to see him sitting at his keyboard, wearing headphones and bobbing his head while glancing at her every now and then. When Braxton had realized she was awake, he bestowed a loving smile on her and came over to the bed in their hotel suite to place a tender kiss on her forehead. Afterward, he unhooked the headphones and played the most beautiful song she'd ever heard him play. Tears were already streaming down her face but when he'd finished, he told her the song was called "Elle." She couldn't help but fall for him even more than she already had, and they topped the morning off by making love again.

And now he had the audacity to play it when she was trying not to be tempted. And he wasn't just playing, he was downright killing her song with so much vigor and emotion as if every single note served a purpose. She shut her eyes tight to suppress the tears. Hearing him caress the keys always put her in some kind of mood depending upon his mood that exuded into each note. This one was screaming a mix of regret and love. He always had a way of expressing himself through his music when he couldn't find the words to say what he was feeling.

She was kind of surprised he'd remembered it. He'd written other songs for her that had appeared on his albums but that one hadn't. She figured he'd forgotten it. Afterward, he played some familiar jazz standards while she soaked in the beautiful scenery in front of her. The blue waves crashing against the sand and the pink-and-orange hues of the sunset were inviting and serene. She took a ton of pictures with her phone and sent them to her head designer.

Upon reentering the cottage, she found Braxton in the kitchen with Chef Jackson whom she recognized from cooking contest shows and some industry parties around New York. One of his assistants approached her with a martini glass filled with an inviting purplish drink.

"Good evening, Ms. Lauren. This is a pomegranate vodka martini."

"Why thank you very much." Elle took a sip and was very impressed with the way the sweet drink had a kick to it as it went down. "This is good. Keep them coming." She turned her attention to Braxton who was wearing a delicious smirk aimed toward her as he watched the chef place two lobsters into a huge pot of boiling water.

"Hey, beautiful. Did you get a lot of pictures?"

Grabbing his martini from the island, he walked over, clutched her hand and led her out to the couch on the veranda in front of the unlit fireplace.

"I did." Pausing, she took a sip of her drink and hoped her voice wasn't shaky when she spoke. "I heard you playing… I didn't think you even remembered 'Elle.'"

He raised a cocky eyebrow and the heat behind his eyes emerged. "I remember you very well. Every single inch of your brown sugar skin."

He strummed his fingers along her arm as if she was a piano. His subtle touch provoked tingles to run rampant through her and end up in her center as if she was being tickled. Then again, that could've been from her Brazilian wax yesterday.

Shifting in her seat to calm down the sensations, she smacked her lips. "I was referring to the song you wrote for me. I figured you'd forgotten how to play it."

He frowned and then said in a sarcastic tone. "Um…I composed it, babe. Of course I remember it."

She giggled. "Yes, but you were like eighteen. That was eons ago, and it wasn't on any of your CDs…not that I was searching for it." She knew as she soon as she had said that, he'd know she was lying.

"I didn't put it on any of them because the song is special to me…like you are. I mean, don't get me wrong, all of my songs are dear to me but… I didn't want to share this one with the world. I wrote it especially for you, Sunshine. And I've played it over the years when I'm feeling a little sentimental or melancholy over you. So, no, I'll never forget it. That would be like forgetting you and what you mean to me. No matter what happens, you'll always be the one that got away. You'll always be the one for me and I'll always regret the day I walked out of your life."

"Really?" she whispered, blinking her eyes rapidly to block the tear that desperately wanted to fall. She refused to let him see her cry again. She was still chastising herself for crying when they had *the talk*.

"Yeah… I know I messed up with you. This may sound sappy, but I didn't know what I had until it was gone. You were my best friend, the love of my life and I hurt you. I will always feel guilty about that." He ran a tender hand down her face and drew her to him, holding her to his chest. "I know you've forgiven me, but I'm still working on forgiving myself."

She snuggled closer to him and wrapped her arms around his waist. "I know you're sorry, Brax. You don't have to feel guilty anymore. I've forgiven you. Trust me, I wouldn't be here if I hadn't. And since you're being transparent, I listen to the song when I'm feeling frustrated over not being with you. I get a little melancholy, as well."

Lifting her chin up, a crafty smize crossed his face. "You still have the copy I made for you?"

She sighed. "I did, but unfortunately a few years

ago as I was taking the CD out of the case and it got stuck. I ended up breaking it by mistake. However, I remember perfectly how it sounds in my head. Every single note. I was so sad when it broke. It was good to hear it again in person."

"Tell you what, I'll record it for you and make a few extra copies just in case."

She kissed his cheek and stood, grabbing her drink from the table. "Thank you. I appreciate that." She had to move away from him. Being with him like that made her forget that they weren't together and her goal for the weekend was to stay strong and resist him. But he was so damn yummy and the martini was giving her the giggles. Giggles around him always ended up with her under him.

"Where are you going?" he asked, patting the cushion on the couch she'd vacated. "I thought we were chatting."

"To freshen up before dinner," she said as the chef's assistant strolled out to set the table for two.

"All right. I'll see you in a few."

Thirty minutes later, Elle stepped back onto the veranda that was lit by only white candles in the fireplace and on the table. Soft jazz played in the background and Braxton had changed into khaki slacks, a blue golf shirt and a black newsboy cap. He stood when she entered and approached him, giving her a warm hug. The fresh scent of soap and cologne filled her senses and his comforting embrace was enough to make her forget her promise to herself. *Be strong, girl. Be strong.* She chanted it over and over in her head as he kissed her hand and then her cheek, keeping her fingers laced with his. His lips on her skin almost knocked her off-kilter, and she continued the chant as he led her to the table. Pulling out her chair, he whispered, "You look sexy in that dress."

Elle glanced down as if she'd forgotten what she was wearing. She'd purposely chosen a simple black polo shirt dress and flip-flops and had styled her hair in a ponytail so he wouldn't be tempted to flirt. She sat and he pushed in her chair.

"You think so?" she asked, surprised, as she unfolded her napkin and set it in her lap. She wanted to look as low-key as possible.

"Elle, it doesn't matter what you wear. You're still a beautiful woman. And with your hair pulled back, I can focus more on your alluring eyes and radiant smile. Goodness I've missed your smile."

"You are too much, Brax." She laughed, reaching for her glass of water. No more martini's for her even though there was a fresh one in hand's reach. "You look nice, as well. I like the cap, but I like your bald head, as well. Very smooth and sexy. It's taken me a moment to get used to it, though. I'm used to your hair."

"I'm glad you find it smooth and sexy. It's time to shave, thus, the cap."

The chef arrived with the lobster sautéed with

shrimp, scallops and vegetables and a risotto with a garlic cream sauce.

"You remembered I love seafood," she said, taking a bite of the dish. "This is delicious, Chef Jackson."

"Thank, Ms. Lauren. Save room for dessert." He skipped out and left them alone.

Braxton dug in as well. They ate in silence for a few minutes and once in a while caught each other staring at one another over the candlelight. It was indeed romantic with the sky completely dark, the candles, and the sultry jazz music playing in the background. She had to break the sensual silence especially when she realized that her feet were intertwined with his under the table. *When did that happen?* It had been a habit of theirs since high school whenever they went out to eat. She didn't want to remove them so she didn't, and continued eating.

"How was your meeting this morning at the club?" She was almost scared to ask that question and even more scared to know the answer. If he bought the building, would he spend more time in New York? A part of her hoped so and her mind started racing with all kinds of questions. *Would he need a place to stay? Would we start to date again exclusively? Would we finally get married?*

Taking a sip of his martini, he finished chewing and dabbed his mouth with a napkin. "It went well. The place needs some renovations, of course, for the vision I have, but my team and I feel that it could definitely work for what I want. It's in a great location. I think it will do well. Plus, it has a small loft apartment above it so I'd have somewhere to stay when I'm in New York."

Well, that's one question answered. Her heartbeat sped up. "So did you put in an offer?"

"My business manager is crunching some numbers and whatnot. Like I said, the place needs some updating, and I'm not paying the asking price unless they plan on doing so. We'll see. I'm excited about it, though."

"What about Memphis?"

"Um…not sure at the moment. Memphis is different. You almost have to be invited if you want a business on Beale Street and there are some stipulations that come with that. I want to own my jazz clubs outright. Like the one in Atlanta. No lease. I own the building, including the four little shops attached on the other side. The business owners pay me."

"Well I'm sure it will work out," she stated in an encouraging tone.

He nodded. "I hope *everything* I want works out the way I want it to."

She noted his smoldering gaze, and she knew he wasn't talking about the club anymore, thus, possibly answering her other questions. "Would you oversee all the renovations or do you have people for that?"

"I'll probably use Megan's crew again if they're

available, but you know I'm a perfectionist so I'd fly back and forth until it's done and help with the hiring along with Chef Jackson. He's one of the investors if we do this thing."

"Oh, that's wonderful. He's quite popular around New York especially after he won the Master Chef Cook-Off last summer. He's been very sought after, doing private parties and such. You two would be a great combination...well, you live in Atlanta, but I guess you'll have to come perform sometimes and check on your investment. After all, it will be called Braxton Chase's Jazz and Dinner Club."

"Mmm-hmm... I'm contemplating about what I'm going to do about that. I can't clone myself or be a hologram so...I have some ideas in mind."

"Two of you? I think one is plenty."

"You can't handle two of me?" he raised a mischievous eyebrow and rubbed his goatee.

Heat flushed her face as she realized the hidden message behind his question. "Um... I'll just stick with the one. And if you were able to clone yourself I'd want the real one, not the clone. You can leave him in Atlanta with the groupies."

"Ahh...so you're admitting you want me, and preferably in New York?"

"That's not what I meant, Brax."

He tightened his grip on her feet wrapped with his, and she managed to swallow down a gulp of her drink. Her mind drifted to being completely intertwined with him. Body. Heart. Soul. Her breathing became stifled for a moment, and she was relieved when Chef Jackson emerged with cheesecake and coffee.

Elle retreated to the couch with her dessert while Braxton went inside momentarily to speak with the chef. His assistants cleaned up the table, leaving the candles lit. Elle glanced through the window and noticed the kitchen was pretty much clean again and the gentlemen were shaking hands.

A vibration from her cell phone in her pocket grabbed her attention. It was a text from Ciara. They'd didn't have a chance to chat much earlier after their marketing meeting because Elle had to catch the Hampton Jitney.

Are you being good?

Elle chuckled at her friend's message and decided to tease her.

No.

Her phone began to ring, which she wasn't surprised by. "Yes, C?"

"What do you mean, no?" Ciara asked in a mother-hen tone.

"Calm down. I was joking."

"Girl, you play too much. You answered, so I

guess that means you're fully clothed. However, did you pack everything necessary just in case?"

"Meaning?"

"Don't be funny. Sexy lingerie, condoms and some lubricant. You know it's been a long time since you had sex. I just want you prepared."

"Trust me. With Braxton I don't need lube. Just looking at him makes me w…" she halted abruptly as he slid on the couch next to her with a curious expression and a half-cocked smile. He hurled something on the table and crossed his leg over his knee. Then he turned to her with his hand resting under his chin and a curious grin as if he were waiting to hear the rest. Not that it mattered. He'd heard way too much already.

"Um…I…have to go." She managed to stutter out.

Ciara shrieked. "Girl, he heard you?"

"Yeahhhhhhh. See you tomorrow." Elle pressed End with a shaky hand and tossed the phone on the cushion between them. Grabbing her cheesecake from the table, she cut off a big piece with her fork, stuffed it in her mouth and chewed slowly.

"You know you'll have to talk sometime." He began eating his cheesecake, too. "Even though I have to say I'm flattered." His cocky, confident expression emerged as he continued to stare her down.

"Mmm-hmm." She avoided eye contact with him, instead focusing on the lit candles in the fireplace before her.

"I was in my room earlier and found a pack of cards. You wanna play?"

"Mmm-hmm." She sipped her coffee and moved to the floor by the fireplace. Anything to get her mind off seducing him, all thanks to Ciara's meddling. Even though Elle had packed all the items in her suitcase.

"It's Truth or Dare cards."

She nearly choked on the last swallow of her cheesecake. "Okay, maybe not." She could only imagine where that would lead.

"Ahh, she speaks. Too late. You already agreed."

"But…"

"Scared?" He challenged.

"Never," she answered boldly. "Bring it."

Striding over to the dinner table, he grabbed the two long stem candles. He then set them on the coffee table. "We need more light."

"You could turn on the ceiling fan light."

"Where's the romance in that? Besides, you've always looked radiant with candlelight shining on you."

Her thoughts drifted back to one of the times she'd visited him on a short holiday break. She'd entered his apartment off campus to a ton of white scented candles. They'd made love right there at the front door before he carried her to the bedroom. The entire time he complimented her on how beautiful she was with the candles shining against her naked flesh.

Ever since then, he'd always have candles lit around her and she suddenly wondered if that was the reason for the white candles in the fireplace. Did he remember? Over the years she'd always wondered if he thought about her in the way she did about him. But she decided he probably didn't because as a woman, she was way more sentimental.

Leaning over the coffee table, he grabbed the deck of cards and began to shuffle them. "So there's thirty cards in the deck. Fifteen truth cards and fifteen dare cards. We pull and ask a question accordingly."

"I know how to play. I had a life after you."

"Touché. Maybe you'll share some of that information with me. I'll be a gentleman and let you go first."

She scooted up to the table and set her plate down. Reaching over to the middle, she pulled a card and flipped it over. "Dare." *Dang it.*

He rubbed his hands together and gave a wicked laugh. "This is going to be good."

"I am *not* showing my ta tas," she said sternly.

"Ah, shucks," he teased, tapping his chin. "Let me think of something else."

She laughed nervously. *Perhaps this was a bad idea.*

"Okay. I dare you to tell me the last time you made love."

Elle wrinkled her nose at his question. She'd rather flash her boobies than to answer that. Of course she could lie, but she didn't know how to lie to him and if she tried, he'd know in an instant.

She was silent for a moment and then whispered. "You."

His face crunched into a frown. "I'm somewhat relieved by that answer because the thought of another man even looking at you, let alone touching and exploring your heavenly body, burns my insides. But, um…you haven't had sex in over a decade?"

"That wasn't the question. I've only ever made love with you. There's a difference. We never had sex."

"Uh-huh. True. So what about sex? I've seen pictures of you on the red carpet with that investment banker cat. Connor something," He paused as a devilish dark twinkle appeared in his eyes and he lowered his voice. "But I know he didn't satisfy you like I did. I know he didn't have you panting for more like you used to with me. He looked like a complete dorky geek. Like his favorite sport is chess or some shit like that."

You are so right, but I will never admit that to you.

"Your turn is up. I answered the dare. Pull a card."

He eyed her for a moment before drawing a card and slamming it on the table as if he had the joker in a Spades tournament. "Truth." He leaned back on the couch. "I'm ready."

"Why haven't you settled down and married yet?

I've seen you on the blogs with drop dead gorgeous women, or are you scared of marriage?"

"Mmm…good question. I could ask you the same thing. Well, some of them were just flings. Kinda hard to have a meaningful relationship when you're always in the studio or touring. The first few years of my career, I stayed on the road. I only saw Atlanta if I was performing there. Plus, a lot of those women wanted to be with Braxton Chase the jazz pianist not *me*. Besides, I've only been in love once. Haven't found anyone quite like you, Sunshine."

"And you never will," she answered matter-of-factly with a cunning smize. "You made your bed."

"I know. And I've been lying in it ever since with no sleep."

She drew a card and turned it over for him to see. "Truth."

"Damn, I wanted a dare." He grabbed the cards and reshuffled the deck.

"If you thought playing this game would get me naked, you're sadly mistaken."

"Baby, I can get you naked without playing this game. What were you telling your friend on the phone? You just look at me and what?" He raised an arrogant eyebrow. "And you need…?"

Heat rushed to her face as she tried to suppress exactly what he was referring to. "Whatever. Ask the question."

"All right. I got a good one, too. At one of my

shows a few years back at Carnegie Hall, I swore I saw you in the audience. I wasn't sure if I was losing my mind or not. The lady had on a short dark blond wig and reading glasses. When the show was over, I searched but I couldn't find her, just the program booklet in the seat. It smelled like expensive perfume…similar to the one you wore at the brunch. Anyway, I've always wondered if that was you since you were in New York at that time. Plus, I know your eyes like I know how to play the piano. There's just some things you never forget."

Elle went silent for a moment as she thought back to that moment in time. She was on an email list for local events around town. Since she'd recently moved to the New Jersey/New York area, she'd wanted to stay abreast of the happenings in the Big Apple. When she'd received the announcement that the Braxton Chase Quartet would be at Carnegie, her heart stopped. Before then, she hadn't thought of him too much. The pain had subsided, and she was happy with her life and her career as a designer for DaVinci Fashions. However, when she'd seen Braxton's picture and the fact that he would be in the city, so close, her heartache had returned. She bought a ticket, regretted it and then contemplated for two weeks whether or not she would attend. She'd thought about confiding in Ciara but decided against it and went with her heart, which had always been her decision maker when it came to him.

At the very last second, Elle had thrown on the wig from a masquerade party she'd attended, grabbed some glasses and bolted to the subway. She'd barely made it to her seat as the show was beginning. But as soon as she had sat, her eyes caught Braxton's as he slightly tilted his head and squinted. Luckily, the house lights had gone off and she was relieved he could no longer see her, even though she had noticed him staring in her direction. As soon as the show ended, she got lost in the crowd of people and skedaddled out of Carnegie and back to the subway. She didn't exhale until she had made it home. The next day, the first of many potted orchids with no note had arrived at her office.

Elle had hoped he wouldn't mention it but now that he had, she might as well be honest. After all it was a "truth" question.

"Yes. It was me."

"I figured it was. Why did you leave? No, run out."

"I wanted to see you play at Carnegie. That had been on your bucket list since we were in middle school and you had attended a show there while at music camp in Boston one summer. I wasn't there for a confrontation. I… I just needed to see you with my own eyes. That's all."

He slid down to the floor where she sat and clutched her hands warmly. "I wish you would've stayed."

"It was your big night, and I didn't want to interrupt it. I just wanted to be there."

"I appreciate that. I was so nervous. My family was in the front row and I was terrified I'd miss a key but then I saw you and I felt better."

"You played well. I was very happy for you. Now pick a card."

Resting his back against the bottom of the couch, he slid a card off the top and placed it on the table. "Dare. And there's nothing I won't do." Winking, he licked his bottom lip as a shiver of electricity jolted through her veins.

"Yes, I remember. I dare you to tell me something you don't want me to know."

"Where's the fun in that?"

"Just answer the dare."

Braxton pondered for a moment before sitting all the way up on the couch, resting his arms on his thighs and leaning in toward her. "I was at your very first fashion show."

Shrugging, she took the last bite of her cheesecake. "I know."

"Oh, you saw me?" he asked with a wrinkled brow. "I was trying to be incognito."

"As I was doing my walk down the runway at the end, I spotted a guy with shades and a cap. I was trying to look away from the flashing lights in my face and caught you leaning on the wall next to the exit door before slipping out of it."

"I just wanted to return the favor. I remember when we were little, you had lined up your stuffed animals and you and my sisters had Barbie dolls walk down the runway while I was forced to play the piano as background music. But seriously, you've wanted this for a long time. I just wanted to be there for your first show."

"Thank you and I didn't force you. You needed to practice anyway. You had a recital coming up."

"I wanted to go outside and play basketball with Preston, not play backup for a Barbie doll fashion show."

"You know you enjoyed it. "She reached over and pulled a card from the stack. "Dare."

"All right. I dare you to let me kiss you on your hot spot."

She rubbed the back of her neck that had missed his lips and tantalizing tongue. The mere thought of him kissing her there would lead to other things. It *always* did. With him she never had any control over rational thinking. If she did, she wouldn't even be with him now. Heck, she wouldn't have even spoken to him at the brunch, danced with him at the auction or had dinner at his restaurant, which was all before they had *the talk*. He'd always been her weakness. Her addiction. *But hey, it was a dare. Right?*

She slid over to where he sat on the floor and rested her body between his legs with her back cozy against his chest. "Okay, but it's not going to turn me on or anything," she stated nonchalantly, and hoped he couldn't hear her heart pound against her chest at one hundred miles per hour.

"Isn't it too late for that?"

Chapter 8

Once again all logic and common sense flew out the window when it came to Braxton, but this time Elle had a good reason or at least that's what she kept telling herself as she sat between his legs waiting impatiently. With the few boyfriends she'd been intimate with she had of course relayed to them her turn-on spots. Her nipples, her thighs, her clitoris and a few points on her neck including where her tattoo resided. However, it was pointless, as none of those areas worked with any of them. She chalked it up to them needing to find their own turn-on spots. But she was wrong as none had succeeded.

Since Braxton had offered or rather dared her to let him kiss the back of her neck, she figured why not. Plus, it would answer a nagging question that had been in her head. Years ago, Ciara had said that the reason no one had figured out how to turn Elle on was because Braxton had programmed every inch on her body as his. She'd laughed it off until she noticed a pattern, and briefly considered that perhaps her best friend was right.

Well, now she was about to find out.

Braxton's arm encircled her waist and pulled her even closer. She didn't think that was possible as she was already pretty snug against him. However, now she could feel his manhood pressed against her bottom through the thin material of her shirtdress.

He ran a finger across the back of her neck that sent her head back against his.

"I take it you like that," he whispered in her ear as the warmth of his tongue brushed against it sending a warm current through her.

"Mmm-hmm." That's all she could muster out as he travelled his tongue along the path to her neck and then it happened. His lips met her skin in the place she'd yearned over the years for him to kiss and savor once more. It was indeed his spot and she had an inkling so was every place else.

"Brax…"

With his free hand he weaved it in the nape of her hair and pushed it up while massaging her head and ravishing her neck at the same time. She clutched his hand that was on her pelvic bone and swung the other one behind her. Knocking off the hat, she held on to his bald head that she'd wanted to run her hands over again ever since the night at her hotel room.

"Is that what you wanted, Elle?" he asked, biting the side of her neck gently.

"Oh, yes. For such a long time. Please don't stop."

"Oh, I'm not. Whatever you want, babe."

Elle turned her head to him and her lips landed on his but she didn't kiss him. "You. Tonight. No strings. Just us. That's what I want."

Braxton didn't answer as his pupils turned jet black and the slight bulge on her butt was no longer slight as it pulsated against her. Removing his hand from her hair, he ran it along her side and down to the hem of her dress, inching it up until her blue lacey boy shorts were displayed.

Turning her around to face him, Braxton's lips hastily captured Elle's as he wound his tongue hard with hers in a deep seductive kiss that she'd craved for years. His arms encircled her frame, and she blissfully welcomed his exploring tongue on her lips as he delved in even more. Tearing his mouth away, he lifted her dress over her head and slid his hand around to her back to unhook her bra, flinging it across the room. Licking his lips, he eyed her breasts before dipping his head as he sucked a nipple into his mouth while massaging the other one. Erotic moans escaped her as she held on to his head and tried to suppress the shudder that was rocking her uncontrollably on him. However, she couldn't help it. She'd missed this man. Missed all the ways he would purposely drive her insane with a passionate high that only he could evoke from her. Tears filled her eyes as she was immersed in Braxton's blazing mouth on her breasts, going back between the two nibbling, biting and sucking them until the pain and pleasure became entangled.

She'd fantasized over the years of how he used to make her feel alive and needed. But the power he possessed at the moment wasn't even close to her fantasy. He was all man now and he handled her as such.

Lifting his head to hers, he closed his lips over hers and in one swoop, laid her on the floor, wrapping her legs around his waist. Holding both hands on the side of her face as his fingers laced in her hair, he stared at her, hovering his lips over hers. Her heart rate increased as her chest fell up and down awaiting his next move.

"I've missed you, Elle. More than I can ever begin to explain, but I promise to show you all night."

"I can't wait."

He awakened every inch of her body as he glided his hand down her side to her hips, finally landing on the spot that had desired and craved him the most. His subtle touch caused exhilarating shocks to rush through her veins. She trembled, and could only imagine what was to come. He slid her boy shorts down and lifted her legs up to take her shorts completely off. His heated gaze roamed over her body with an intensity that signified their foreplay would be brief. He was hungry for her, and she couldn't wait to be devoured.

Braxton kissed her gently at first as his hand rubbed her in the same rotating manner and on the same beat. As he deepened his tongue, his hand moved down a tad, slipping a finger into her slick canal. Moaning out, her back arched up off the floor and he captured her lips once more. But this time he kissed her with an intensity, as if she were all his once again. Claiming possession over them and over her heart and soul.

"I missed you, Brax. I need you so bad." She grinded her hips with his fingers. "Please let's just skip the foreplay. I know you want me right now, Maestro."

"And I do. I just wanted to make sure you're ready for all of me."

Her breath stifled as she remembered what it *all* was. "I'm ready." She gulped a tad, as she was now overly anxious to have him.

Lifting her up off the floor, he carried her inside the house and to his bedroom. Laying her on top of the comforter, he stood next to the bed and began to unbutton his shirt, exposing all of his glorious, chocolate skin and that's when she saw it. His tattoo. It was supposed to be one of her truth questions during the game, but she never had the chance to ask. As he slid out of his slacks, she stood and ran a finger over the treble clef entwined with her name.

"You still have it," she said softly.

"And you still have yours."

Pulling her to him, he unleashed a sweet, unhurried sensual kiss that caused a sigh of relief to escape her. She'd wondered for years whether he still had the tattoo, or if he'd had it removed so he wouldn't think of her. She couldn't help but wonder what his other girlfriends had said about him having a tattoo of her name, but now wasn't the time. Now she needed to exhale and release all of the pent-up fervor for him that had been buried deep inside her heart.

"Make love to me," she whispered on his lips and ran her hand down to the band of his boxer shorts and tugged them down. "I can't wait any longer."

"With pleasure."

Braxton stood briefly, roaming his eyes over her sexy body, soaking in her the essence. He couldn't believe he was here with her. He'd daydreamed of being one again with her, feeling her brown sugar skin under him and listening to her soft purrs that would escalate with each kiss or stroke that he'd given her. Making love to her had always been fulfilling. With other women it had been just to get himself off and vice versa. However, with Elle his concentration had always been to satisfy her and she did the same for him. Their connections: heart, body and soul had always been in sync and now he wanted to remind her of that and show her just how much he missed her.

Before joining her, he reached into the side drawer of his nightstand and pulled a packet out and tossed it on the bed. She raised an eyebrow and twisted her lips to the side. "Oh, so you just knew we were going to make love, Maestro?"

Climbing on top of her, he kissed her deeply, delving his tongue into her mouth and initiating a wicked dance with hers as the purrs he loved to hear erupted from her throat.

"And you didn't bring any?"

"Um… I did just in case. Now please put it on," she pleaded in between their mouths. "Please." Her hips rose up to him and he had to restrain himself from thrusting inside of her. But he had his rules and that wouldn't change until he got married…hopefully to her.

"Wait, baby." He reached over to where the packet had fallen, opened it and rolled it on all the while she was breathing with anticipation.

Wrapping her legs around his waist, he kissed her as he slowly entered while her moans and breathing rose with each inch. She wiggled her hips until he was all the way in and he stared at her for a moment, holding still until she was calm.

"Are you all right?" he asked, kissing her forehead.

"Yeah…just…um…did you grow some?"

"No, babe. You're just a little extra snug."

She smiled. "Mmm, but we still fit perfectly together."

"Always, my love."

When Braxton moved a little, her eyes fluttered shut and her head lifted off the pillow. Clutching his shoulders, she moved her hips up and he began to slide in and out of her at a steady momentum. He became engrossed in her body and mind as he always had when they became one. They were in absolute harmony with each other. Their lips, limbs, joyful cries and hearts were tangled together as the fervor of their lovemaking amplified. Her muscles squeezed around him pulling and constricting tighter with each thrust. She wrapped her legs tight around his neck and he held her hands on the comforter as he dove in more and more. Her body shuddered hard against his and she squirmed and wiggled under him as her orgasm tore through her body. The incoherent yet seductive sounds she made were music to his trained ears. Her ardent cries aroused a feral reaction from him. Never had a woman felt so damn good before, including her, because this time was different from all the rest. His pent-up need for her was spilling through his soul and he couldn't even fathom how he'd spent his years without his sweet Elle. As her next orgasm neared, it wasn't long before her walls began to clutch around him once more to an excruciating desire-filled earthquake. He lost all the control he had tried to keep composed as he shook against her, holding on to her for dear life.

As their breathing calmed down, he rolled off her but held her in his embrace. He wasn't ready to let go. Ten years without her was long enough and he decided then that he had to do everything in his power to make her his once more.

Resting her head on Braxton's hard chest, Elle swirled her finger along the treble clef and her name while he placed tender kisses on her forehead. They were both happily sated after their lovemaking sessions and too exhausted to move. She'd used muscles that hadn't been active in a long while, and she was completely sore all over. Being with him again had been pure ecstasy and triggered so much pent-up passion and desire for him that she was scared she'd break him in half for holding on to him so tight. She couldn't help it. She'd missed him and he needed to know just how much.

Kissing his collarbone, she sat up on her elbow and stared down at him. Reaching his hand up, he cupped her chin and pulled her down for a sweet kiss.

"Hi there," he whispered. "I thought you were asleep."

"No. My eyes were just closed. I was enjoying listening to your breathing and your heart beat."

He smiled knowingly and kissed her again. "You used to say my heartbeat was your favorite sound."

"It still is."

"It says your name."

Giggling, she relaxed her head back on his chest and a thought crossed her mind.

"Sooooooo…not that I really want to know about your relationship life after me, but how have you managed to not have my name removed from your chest? You've had other girlfriends and the serious one that I saw you on the red carpet with at the Grammys and a few other awards shows that year. None of them ever asked you to laser it off?" she asked curiously.

"Mmm…yeah, but I always told them that it was a painful reminder of hurting you. Some of them just didn't care because they were with Braxton Chase, the jazz artist. The alleged "serious one" you're referring to demanded I have it removed and replaced with her name. I nearly laughed when she said it."

"Um…that makes sense, Braxton. No woman wants to see another woman's name tattooed on her man's body."

"Yeah, she kept saying I had to do it before we got married."

Her body tensed against his, and he rubbed her back, which calmed her down a smidge. "I didn't know you were engaged."

"I wasn't. But in her mind we were getting married. I guess she figured she'd lasted longer than the others."

"So why didn't you marry her, playboy?" she asked in a teasing manner.

"I'm not a playboy and I didn't marry her for a lot of reasons, but the main one was I didn't love her. I tried, I really did, but something was missing. It never felt right with her or anyone...except with you, Sunshine. I couldn't love another woman because I'd left my heart with you."

Sitting all the way up, she threw her leg over him and straddled his stomach. She leaned over to give him a single smooch, but he sunk his tongue in and bestowed a hard yet sensual kiss on her lips. He weaved his hands in her hair pulling her deeper to him. She knew her hair was just plain hideous after all their sweating, but she didn't care. She was where she wanted to be. In his arms. In their world. That is until her back stiffened with pain and she couldn't move.

"What's wrong?"

"I think it's safe to say you blew my back out, Maestro. I'm stuck."

"I'm sorry, babe." He turned her over gently and propped a pillow under her head. "You want some painkillers?"

She tried to suppress a laugh at his concern but couldn't hold it in, even though her sore muscles cracked at the same time. "No, sweetie, it's a good thing. Perhaps, you can do it again before we leave the Hamptons."

"Oh, with pleasure, but in the meantime how about a hot bath in that huge soaking tub with me." A devilish smile emerged across his features as he scooped her in his arms and carried her to the master bathroom.

"I wouldn't want it any other way."

Moments later she sat in between his legs, resting her back comfortably against his chest as the warm water and bubbles filled the tub.

"Riddle me this, Elle." He travelled a finger along her neck. "Why do you still have *my* initials? I'm sure your so-called boyfriends had to have seen them and asked what they meant. That nerdy jerk, I mean gentleman, didn't inquire?"

"So-called boyfriends? You're funny. Anyway, yes they did, and I gave the same answer each time. The BC stands for beautiful and confident. I told them it was a fashion thingy. They all bought it, too. I even used it for one of my ad campaigns."

"I saw that but it never occurred to me why. You didn't answer the first question. Why didn't you have it lasered off?"

"Because it stands for bold and confident, like me." *Because I still love you and couldn't bring myself to have it done. Twice.*

"You mean beautiful and confident, don't you?" he asked with a mischievous snicker.

"Whatever." She turned around and slid to the other side of the tub while playfully splashing water on him in the process. Grabbing her feet, he tickled the bottoms, which released a loud laugh from her. She hated that he remembered she was ticklish pretty much all over.

"Stop tickling me before I kick you somewhere by mistake under all these bubbles. Even though, I may want it again later on."

Elle flicked bubbles on him and Braxton immediately let go. She drew her knees up to her chest while calming down her hysterical laughter.

"You have a point, Sunshine." He dragged her feet back to him and set them on either side of his waist. "So what's on the Elle Lauren Designs schedule for next week?"

She sighed at the long list of things on her plate. "Getting ready for a new ad campaign, a fashion show for my new collection, my new perfume, and finding time to sleep and eat. Did I mention drink wine?" she asked sarcastically even though it was true. The next few months leading up to the change of seasons were filled with nothing but work and she wouldn't have it any other way.

"You have a busy schedule. Speaking of perfume. What's the name of the one you wore to Carnegie Hall? It's the same one you wore to the brunch. I couldn't forget the scent. That's when I figured I was correct all along about you attending the concert."

"Funny you mention it. A month or so before the concert, I'd attended a perfume class with some friends. It was just a mixture of oils I put together. I still make it and wear it. And now it's going to be the first perfume under my design company. It's called Elle. It will be out this fall."

"That would explain why whenever I passed perfume counters and smelled the samples I could never find it. Are you thinking about doing a men's companion fragrance?"

"We're looking to release it sometime before Father's Day next year," She glided back to her original spot between his legs. Wrapping his arms around her, she nestled against him once more and interweaved her legs with his.

"Are your muscles feeling better now?" he asked after a few moments of silence.

"I'm fine." She paused to yawn eliciting one from him. "I work out and do yoga, but I guess there were a few parts that hadn't been worked out in awhile. However, I had fun doing so."

"Well, I aim to please."

Sucking the side of her neck, he slid his hand between her legs and rotated a slow, sensual finger around her clit. Soft moans emerged from her throat as he sped up the tempo and her sounds reached higher levels with each passing second. Her hips began to move in sync and the quick orgasm that approached ruptured through her. Closing her eyes, she slumped against him and exhaled to calm down her breathing. She yawned again and pressed her body even closer against his as he wrapped his arms tight around her and kissed the top of her head.

"Sleepy, Sunshine?"

"I am, but I'm enjoying our time together. I don't want it to ever end."

"It doesn't have to."

"Um…yes it does, or we'll be prunes soon." Giggling, she sat up and reached for a towel on the ledge as he popped her on the bottom.

"I meant us, Elle."

She froze at his words. While she was having a remarkable time with him, she still wanted to take it day by day and mentioning anything remotely that sounded like forever wasn't on her list for discussion. There was a still a part of her that had doubts.

Standing, she stepped out as he followed suit. Braxton took the towel from her and began to dry her off. After they were both dry, he lifted her once again and carried her back to the bed. Moments later she was at peace, enclosed in his protective arms like a caterpillar in a cocoon as they faced each other. She watched as his eyelids became heavy and closed, only to shoot open again as he'd release a sleepy grin and then repeat the pattern over again. As her eyes finally shut, she nestled her head into the crook of his neck and fell asleep with a fulfilled smile.

Chapter 9

Elle snuggled in the warmth of the down comforter
that she'd wrapped around her naked body moments
before when she'd begun to feel a bit cold from the
air conditioner. She'd been warm all night against
Braxton's chest, kissing it and running her fingers
along his tattoo. They'd wake up for a moment to
kiss or mumble terms of endearment to each other
before falling back into a light slumber. Elle almost
didn't want to fall asleep. She'd been at peace staring
into his soulful, warm eyes as he'd tenderly rubbed
her damp hair or placed light kisses on her forehead.
However, now that she was half-awake, it dawned on
her that she was no longer intertwined with his body.

Jolting all the way up, she jerked her head to his

side of the bed only to find it empty. Squinting her eyes as the vast picture window on the left side of the room filled her vision with sunlight, she swung her stiff legs out of the bed. She then headed toward the bathroom while stretching her arms all the way above her head. Upon entering, she noticed Braxton's hair clippers on the counter. His cologne mixed with fresh soap filled the room. After a refreshing shower, she trudged to the closet and perused her outfits but she didn't feel like getting dressed quite yet. She ran her fingers along his clothes and decided to snatch one of his dress shirts from the hanger. The smell of food touched her nose and she scampered out of the bedroom and into the kitchen to find Braxton in jeans and a fraternity T-shirt.

"Good morning, Chef Maestro." Wrapping her arms around his waist, she nuzzled her head in his shoulder and peaked over to see what he was cooking. Bacon was frying in one pan and scrambled eggs with cheese, already done, sat on the back burner. A plate of raisin toast was on the counter with mouth-watering melted butter. He knew her well.

"Good *afternoon*, Sunshine."

"Afternoon?" she asked, puzzled, turning her head toward the microwave clock.

"Yep, it's a little after twelve."

"How long have you been up?"

"About four hours. I've practiced, spoken with my

business manager, answered emails and updated my social media accounts."

"Well you've had a productive morning but why didn't you wake me? I hate sleeping past eight."

"Because you needed your rest. I wore you out last night." He turned his head slightly to her and kissed her cheek. "Remember?" he reminded her with a pompous smirk.

"Whatever." She playfully pinched his arm and proceeded to the coffeemaker where an oversized mug sat along with sugar and hazelnut cream. "So no burnt bologna sandwiches and your version of sunny-side up, i.e., completely raw eggs?" she joked, pouring her coffee and then leaning against the counter while he made their plates.

"Hey, I was a fantastic chef at age ten," he said as he carried their plates to the kitchen table. "You ate it, didn't you?"

"I just didn't want to hurt your feelings." She winked and slid into the chair. "This looks great. You know I love more cheese than eggs. Glad you remembered."

"I remember everything about you, my love. And I was impressed by the new things I learned last night."

Blushing, she lowered her head and took a bite of the eggs that were perfect. "So what time do you have to leave for the festival?"

"In about an hour. What time are your girls coming to pick you up?" he inquired, referring to Ciara and Mya.

"Around two." She glanced at him as he typed on his laptop before closing the lid. "So you update your own social media accounts?"

"Most of the time. I like to personally answer as many of my fans' comments as possible. My assistant takes care of the club and the band accounts, though. I'm assuming you don't."

"No. Not really. I check on them, but Mya and another assistant handle that. Plus, I'm not really into social media on a personal level, but it's great for business." She shrugged and took a bite of her raisin toast.

"Sooooo you don't have just a social media account that's not associated with your company?"

"I did, still do I suppose. But work got hectic so Mya handles that one, as well. I check it out and post sometimes." She sipped her coffee and peered at him over the mug. "Why?"

An arrogant smile dashed across his face and fear crept in as her pulsed race. She had a notion as to why he was asking. She'd been caught.

Biting into a piece of bacon, he leaned back in his chair. After dabbing his mouth with a napkin, he took a sip of his orange juice. The prolonging of his answer agitated her.

"A few years ago I'd received a notification that Elle Lauren liked one of my pictures and then just as quick as it was liked, the notification was gone. Was that you or Mya?"

Sighing, she remembered the incident well. Megan and Syd had both liked the picture in question. Since she was friends with them, the picture had showed up on Elle's timeline feed as she was scrolling through absently one night. It was a very smooth and sexy photo of him sitting behind a baby grand on the stage at his jazz club. In the moment, she hadn't been mad at him. She had been proud of him because the caption stated the club was opening its doors the next day. She'd traveled a finger along his handsome face and somehow made the mistake of clicking Like. The tears clouding her vision may have had something to do with the mistake, as well. When she'd realized it, she quickly clicked Unlike and said a little prayer that Braxton wasn't alerted because it happened so fast. After that, she gave Mya permission to take over her personal account to avoid any more mishaps.

Reaching for her mug, she cleared her throat and took a sip. "This sure is some good coffee. Did you grind the beans yourself? It's very fresh." She took another sip. "Mmm, so much better than instant."

"Elle?"

"Okay, fine. I can admit that it was me, but don't act like you haven't checked out my social media accounts either, Mr. Braxton Chase. Mya charged into my office like a mad woman with her laptop to show me you'd liked several of my pictures from an interview I did with *Modern Bride* last spring." She remembered that day well and had simply shrugged it off in front of Mya. However, inside Elle was a wreck and couldn't focus for the rest of the day.

"I didn't take mine back, either. I wanted you to know I liked them...no, loved them. You were sexy as hell in that blue dress, woman. I was like damn, she's fine, and you were wearing my favorite color." He scooted back from the table, grabbed his dishes and then set them on the counter next to the sink. "I was thinking you wore it for me."

"You're crazy." She tossed her fork on her empty plate. "Don't you need to get ready for the jazz fest?"

"Rushing me?"

"No, but you hate being late." She came to stand in front of him and encircled his neck with her arms, standing up on her toes to kiss him. "Breakfast was delish. Thanks, babe. I'll clean the kitchen."

"Yeah, you're right. Just not ready to leave you." Squeezing her bottom, he drew her closer and lowered his lips to hers in a deep, slow kiss. "I don't know how to keep my hands and lips off you. And you have the audacity to look adorable in my shirt," he said as he unbuttoned it to reveal that she wasn't wearing anything under it. Picking her up, he carried her to the couch in the great room and laid her down as he slid his body over hers. "Just one quickie for the road?"

"You have to go to work."

Catching a nipple with his lips, he teased it until it hardened. She held on to his head as a pleasure groan emerged from her. The man knew all of her turn-ons and intended to drive her insane with his knowledge.

"You don't know what a quickie is, Maestro."

"You're right. I love to savor you," he groaned, sinking his mouth over her breast once more.

Laughing out loud at his comment, she couldn't refuse him or his tongue.

After Braxton left for the jazz fest, Elle grabbed her laptop and cell phone and decided to go over her schedule for the next month. With her new line releasing soon she had a million and one things to do. But her minivacation to the Hamptons with Braxton was a much needed break from her hectic life. The ringing of her cell broke her concentration of browsing pictures of purses the research team had sent that morning to get feedback on. It may have been a holiday but she still had work to do. Glancing at the phone, she saw a picture of her mom and answered happily. Then she quickly remembered she hadn't told her parents about Braxton being back in her life.

"Hey, Mom!"

"Hello, my dear. Is this a bad time?"

"No, just going over some things. Is everything okay?"

"Oh, yeah. We're headed to Pensacola Beach to

see the Blue Angels perform. Your dad is driving so we just wanted to check on you. Haven't heard from you in a few days."

Elle sighed. Because she was an only child, she tried to check on them at least every other day. They were in their early sixties and still quite active. She wanted to make sure they were fine considering they lived so far away from her. She'd tried convincing them to move to the Hamptons on a few occasions and even told them that she'd pay for it. But they'd insisted on Destin because it had been their favorite spot to vacation when she was growing up and they preferred the beautiful snow-white sand and the Gulf of Mexico.

"I'm well, Mom. Just preparing for the new line."

"Oh, yes. I'm so excited that you're finally doing clothes for the everyday woman now."

"You inspired it, Mom, since you said you can't wear my evening gowns everywhere. You can wear this line of clothing to church, your book club meetings or wherever. I'll send you all the pieces before the line hits the stores. There's also purses and shoes so you'll be set for the fall and winter, too, since it doesn't get that cold in Destin."

"Thanks, love…huh… oh, wait. Your dad is asking what about him. He can't wear his tuxedos all the time even though he's very handsome in them, which you know. I have to pinch myself sometimes."

Elle laughed. Her dad always asked that. "Kiss him for me and tell him I have cologne in the works."

"Perfect. So what are you doing for the Fourth of July? You're not all alone in that big house in New Jersey are you?" Her mother asked with concern. "You could've hopped on a private plane and come to Destin."

Elle sighed. Her parents still worried about her living alone as if she were a teenager and not in her thirties and the CEO of her own company. They even suggested she inquire about a roommate when she first purchased the mansion a few years ago. "No, actually I'm in the Hamptons for the next few days."

"Oh, with Ciara and her hubby?" Her mom asked in an upbeat manner. She thought of Ciara and even Mya as her other daughters.

"Um…no, not exactly. Ciara is in town, though. She'll be here in about an hour to pick me up for the jazz festival. Mya, too."

"Oh, so Mya's with you? Tell her I said hello."

"No… I'm with a friend." *Dang it. I should've just lied because now here comes the twenty questions that I don't want to answer.*

"A friend? Male friend? Connor perhaps?"

"No, Mother. Connor and I are never ever getting back together." Her parents had liked Connor way more than she ever had.

Elle pondered whether or not to tell her mother it was Braxton. Even though her parents had remained friends with the Chases, they still weren't exactly fond of Braxton.

"Oh, so someone new?" Her mother's voice went up an octave. Lately she'd been talking about grandchildren and puppies for some reason. But Elle kept reminding her mom she needed a man first for children, and as far as puppies were concerned, she was allergic.

"Not exactly. It's Braxton Chase." She held her breath as she heard nothing but silence for a few moments.

"Braxton? The Braxton that left my baby and doesn't deserve her. That Braxton Chase?"

"Do we know another one?"

"Don't get smart, young lady," she snapped. "Why are you seeing him again?"

"I'm not… We just kinda ran into each other in Atlanta when I went to meet with a celebrity client. Megan invited me to a sorority brunch and it was at his jazz club. But I'm fine, Mom. I was finally able to talk with him after all this time and it felt good to get it all out." Her mind traveled back to last night and the hour before. She definitely got it all out, but decided not to share that tidbit of information with her mother. "Say something, Mom."

"I'm just shocked and so is your dad."

Now she regretted telling her mom because she wasn't sure where her and Braxton's relationship was headed. "I'm not back with Brax."

"Your Dad is pissed and so am I. That man just up and left you and he almost cost me my friendship with my best friend."

"I know, but you don't have to worry. I'm fine. We're just… I don't know. Getting to know each other again. That's all." *On all levels.*

"Baby girl, be careful. I know you loved him, you've been crazy about him since you were a little girl. I know he feels horrible for hurting you but that doesn't mean you have to get back with him." Her mother paused. "Do you still love him?"

"I never stopped, but I don't know if that's enough to be with him. He's sincerely sorry and he still loves me but I'm not going to jump in with my eyes half-closed. I promise, you and Dad don't have to worry about me even though I know you will."

"Of course we are. You're our baby. You may be one of the top wedding dress designers running a half-billion-dollar company, but to us, you're still our baby. We love you, and I just hope you know what you're doing with Braxton, but then again you've always made the best decisions."

"Thank you, Mom. I gotta run and get ready. Ciara will be here soon."

"Oh, yes. For the jazz festival. I'm assuming Braxton is performing?"

"Yes…yes he is."

"Okay, have fun."

"Thank you and you two have fun watching the Blue Angels."

Elle plopped her head on the table. She hadn't intended to tell her parents yet, but at least they weren't as upset as she thought they'd be. That was one hurdle out of the way. Now if she could fully trust that Braxton would never leave her again, she would consider being his again. This time forever.

"Hey, diva!" Ciara greeted as Elle slid into the back of the Escalade next to her. "Love your dress. Did you steal that sample from the warehouse?" she asked teasingly, running her eyes over it.

Elle chuckled as the driver closed her door. "Um…no. I can't steal what I own. Besides, this is the irregular one," she pointed out, smoothing the pleats of the yellow knee-length dress, two of which had been sewn crooked. "The sample is still hanging with the others." She tossed her tote bag on the floor next to Ciara's bag and noticed her MacBook Air sticking out.

Elle's face scrunched with concern as she buckled her seat belt. "I know you didn't bring your laptop to the festival. We're supposed to be eating food that our trainer is going to make us pay for next week and drinking strawberry margaritas."

Mya turned around from the passenger seat in the front with a condescending smirk. "Yep. We've been working since the ride over on the Hampton Jitney," she said in a flippant manner. "Everyone else was having a grand time and Ciara wanted to go over the graphic ideas for the new labels."

Ciara mumbled "fire her" under her breath to Elle. "I will do it for you."

"Fine, but not during Braxton's set." Elle pulled out her cell phone to send him a text message that she was on her way. She twirled a strand of her hair around her finger when he returned the text with a selfie of him wearing a delicious smile. Instantly reminding her of their time on the couch, then in the shower before he'd left for the festival. She snapped a selfie of herself blowing a kiss and sent it back.

"Mmm… I see why you asked me to bring a floppy hat." Twisting her lips to the side, Ciara reached back to the third row and grabbed the hat.

Elle knew her best friend wanted answers as she eyed her carefully over her shades and tapped her sandal-clad foot.

Pressing the button for the soundproof partition between the front seats so the driver and Mya wouldn't hear, Elle placed the hat over her lion's mane, as Braxton had called it while she was blow-drying her hair after their shower. Afterward she'd brushed it in a low side ponytail to hide the right side of her neck that had become Braxton's favorite spot to nibble on last night, which had resulted in a few red marks.

"Wasn't your hair perfectly and professionally laid

yesterday in elegant cascading curls? Maryza would curse you out in Spanish if she saw the travesty on your head. Please tell me you didn't go swimming and if so, did you at least put a conditioner in your hair for protection? You have a relaxer."

"I didn't go swimming…" Elle tried to compress a smile but a huge, mischievous one appeared anyway.

Ciara slid her shades down and peaked over them. "Uh-huh. Well according to the love bite I see peeking out from the side of your neck where you so strategically tried to place your hair, it seems you've been a naughty girl." She waved a finger at her. "And I'm happy for you, girlfriend."

"I wouldn't say naughty…okay, maybe so. It just happened. I wasn't planning it that way. My goal for the weekend was to catch up on our lives and spend some time getting to know each other again. Braxton had Chef Jackson prepare a wonderful seafood dinner that we ate by candlelight on the veranda with sensual jazz playing in the background. Everything was the opposite of what I had planned in my head."

"Humph, seems like ol' Braxton had a romantic evening planned for his Sunshine and he succeeded."

"We were playing Truth or Dare and the next thing I know…well, you can see the rest." Elle pointed to the red mark and a silly high school girl giggle followed.

"Yes, Truth or Dare can lead to that and you did more than catch up. You made up for lost time."

"Girl, I'll say. I'm sore all over, but it was well worth it."

"You're glowing. So are you two back together?"

"Yes and no. I don't know." She paused, shaking her head. "He wants to be, that's for sure, but the thought scares me. I mean it's been ten years, he's back in my life and we just pick up where we left off? Is that possible? I know you and your honey had broken up and are now happily married, but it was only a year's breakup. You practically talked to the man every other day and even had a few backslides. I haven't spoken to Braxton in ages. What if he's no longer the man I fell in love with? I mean, so far he's the same just more mature and sure of himself. I just don't want to rush anything. But at the same time, it still feels right like it always had. Like we're perfect for each other. Like he's still my soul mate, and my best friend."

"Girl, I don't think time matters. If you two still love each other, I believe that is the key. I know you never stopped loving him." Ciara reached over and patted her hands wearing a warm, reassuring smile.

Sighing, Elle stared out the window as she processed her friend's words. She still loved Braxton. There was no denying that. And while he was the same attentive and caring guy he always had been with her—and the extra sexy swag and commanding presence was a plus—a part of her feared he'd leave her again. However, he seemed more grounded and extra confident now. Ten years ago, they were young, fresh out of grad school and both had a lot of growing up to do. Even though that still didn't justify his not showing for their big day. Now they were both successful in their careers and had led happy lives overall without the other. Though now she couldn't see herself being with anyone but Braxton. Like him, she hadn't married for the same reasons he'd hadn't. Her heart belonged to him and even though she'd tried to love again, it wasn't the same soul connection. He'd been her one true love and no matter how hard she fought her mixed emotions, her heart would win every time.

Chapter 10

Braxton strolled out to the beach in front of the house where Elle was waiting for him. He'd returned from the jazz fest earlier that evening, showered and napped with her in his arms. When he'd awakened, there was a note on her pillow that read she was outside on the beach. The full moon was huge and high in the sky that evening, shining a tranquil light on the water and on her. Perched on a blanket, she was on the phone arguing with someone. He could tell it was work related and decided to sit next to her and not go with his original plan of settling in behind her and laying a kiss on her neck. She blessed him with a beautiful smile when he approached, and held a finger signaling to give her a moment. He'd noticed a bottle of wine chilling in an ice bucket and wineglasses along with a tray of finger foods. Pouring them both a glass, he handed her one, and she leaned over and kissed his cheek while still ranting on the phone.

It had been long, hot day at the festival but he was elated to see Elle in the audience cheering him on as she had since his very first recital when he was six years old. During their time apart, he missed spotting her amongst the crowd. She'd always been supportive and encouraging even when he had doubted himself or missed a note. She'd say, "No one noticed but you, babe. You were absolutely perfect," and then top it off with a huge, comforting hug or kiss.

Tossing her phone on the blanket, Elle sipped her wine and laid her head in his lap, gazing up at him with a sweet smile that touched his soul. Sometimes he couldn't believe she was back in his life and that he'd been given a second chance to make her his once again. He bowed his head and placed a kiss to her succulent lips.

"Hi there, beautiful." He held his hands tenderly on her face and kissed her again. But this time he delved deeper, mingling his tongue erotically with hers just so he could hear her soft purrs. She placed her hands over his, interweaving her fingers with his and pulling him deeper into her mouth. He felt her grip loosen slightly when some passersby walking their dog yelled, "Get a room." She giggled, and he lifted his lips from hers. He really didn't care who watched him kiss the woman he loved but it was a public beach and nowadays people took pictures and videos with their phones. He didn't want either of them on the gossip blogs—especially not Elle.

She sat up and popped a strawberry into her mouth. "You finally got up."

"You could've woken me up."

"Nah...you were snoring so hard. You needed your rest. You've been functioning off adrenaline all day, babe," she said, rubbing his back.

"I'm used to it and I don't snore," he said through gritted teeth.

"Apparently some of your groupies over the years have lied to you, Maestro, because you do when you're exhausted. But seriously, you need to relax. It's good to give your brain and body a break sometimes. I know that's hard for you to do but now that the jazz fest is over, you and I are going to spend the next few days chillaxing and doing absolutely nothing."

Braxton was stumped at her suggestion. Rest? Relax? Traveling out of town was a break for him despite the fact he still had meetings and the festival to attend.

"Um...does that include practicing?"

"For?" She sipped her wine and eyed him curiously over the glass.

"Nothing in particular. I have to play every day

though, and I'm composing some new music that I need to work some kinks out of."

"One hour."

"One? I need three at least."

"Two hours." Climbing on top of him, she nibbled his ear and pressed her breasts hard against his chest. "And I promise to make the other twenty-two hours *very* special."

"Mmm-mmm, I like the sound of that."

"I'm sure you do."

He cupped her bottom and followed it with a smack.

"You certainly have been popping my butt a lot lately. I don't remember you doing that before."

"Wasn't that damn plump before." He popped it again and pulled her closer to him so she could feel the beginning of his erection.

"Blame my personal trainer for that. Squats and leg lifts."

"Tell your personal trainer I said thank you."

"You're so silly."

Her phone cell beeped and she reached over to grab it. She read the message with a slight grimace and tossed the phone back on the blanket.

"Everything okay?"

"Yes. It was just the end of an argument I've been having with Kirk, my fashion show coordinator. We aren't seeing eye to eye on the type of models I want. He sent me pictures earlier of girls who look like they haven't eaten in weeks. And yes, I know that's the norm for print ads and shows, but he also knows I cater to women of all sizes and heights. My collections range from petite to plus-size and I want all representations. He knows this. Everyone can't be a perfect size two and who's to say that's even perfect? I don't and he knows that. So now he's saying he's holding another model audition tomorrow and will send me pictures afterward so I can choose."

Wrapping his arms around her waist, he pulled her on top of him to lie on the blanket. "Awww...so you'll be working, too?"

"Well...no... I'll be looking at pictures to approve. Not really work." She wrinkled her nose and then rubbed it against his.

"Still work, my lady."

"Fine. I'll only look at the pictures during your two-hour practice period. By the way, when is that?"

"No set time. Just when we have some down time."

"Okay."

"It's nice out here, isn't it?" he asked after a few moments of silence when a cool breeze blew over them.

"It is. I love how the moon is full and shining in the sky, and we're finally under it together..."

Her voice trailed off in a quiet manner as she sighed and sat all the way up on him, resting her palms on his chest as he held her by the hips. Her dress rose to her thighs, and he could see her lacy black panties that sat perfectly over his erection. It had begun when she had nibbled his ear but now he was ready for more. However, he noted the solemn expression on her face. Knowing the reason behind it, he reached up and caressed her cheek and a melancholy smile appeared.

"Are you okay, babe?"

"Mmm-hmm." She glanced away.

"I know you're lying and I know what's wrong. Let it out. That's why I'm here."

Kissing his palm, she gripped his hand. "I remember when we were both preparing for college and you had to go a week before me. We were sitting on my front porch before you got ready to leave. I was crying as if you'd died and I would never see you again. The moon was full and beautiful like it is tonight. You said whenever I miss you, just look up at the sky at the moon because we could both see it at the same time. Sometimes we'd talk on the phone and do so. But after we broke up, I still couldn't help but look at the moon and think of you and wonder if you were looking at it, too? If you were even thinking about me?"

Her voice cracked and he sat up, drawing her hard to him. Wiping a few tears away from her cheeks, he kissed her softly. "Yes, every single time, babe. Every single damn time." He rested his forehead on hers and held her tight as her body stiffened against him.

"I just still can't believe you left me. Braxton you have to promise to never do that again if you're truly serious about us." She squeezed his shoulders hard. "Do you have any idea what it's like to not be with the person you love? It hurts like hell, and I've hated every minute of it and sometimes, I hated you. So if you're serious about getting me back, don't eff up. If you do, I'll never forgive you or myself for trusting you again."

Braxton listened to her and he knew she meant what she'd said. He'd been given a second chance with her, and he wasn't going to blow it.

"I'm sorry that I put you through all of that, but I promise you, I'm not going anywhere, beautiful."

She didn't answer but instead slid off him and lay down on her back gazing up at the sky in silence. Lying next to her, he grabbed her hand and kissed it gently before placing it over his heart. He held it snug and turned to watch her as she continued to stare. She didn't look at him but she squeezed his hand and whispered. "I'm okay. Just give me a minute."

About thirty minutes later they retired to the house and back to almost the same position they were in on the beach but this time in the bed. She'd been quiet for the most part except about who was carrying what inside. After awhile she finally turned toward him and intertwined her legs with his. Settling her head on his shoulder, she whispered, "Are you asleep?"

"Nope. Gazing at you, Sunshine."

"Oh. It's so dark in here. I can't see your eyes."

"Shall I light a candle?"

"No. Are you sleepy?"

"A little. Why?"

"Nothing. I just want you to rest, Braxton. You've had a long day."

"I'm fine. Trust me, I've had longer. Besides, you're in my arms and I can't think of any other way to sleep."

"Good night, Maestro."

"Sweet dreams, Elle."

The next evening after returning from an all-day Jet Ski and parasailing adventure, or rather nightmare according to Elle, they ate dinner prepared by Chef Jackson. Then continued the night with a cuddle session on the couch watching the movie *Brown Sugar*.

"I can't believe you're crying," Braxton said as the movie ended. He strolled to the DVD player to eject the disc, placing it back in its case.

"It's such a sweet love story. I cry every time. They've known each other and were best friends since they were children like us. It kind of reminds me of you, except they never dated. But still, at the end, they realized they were meant to be." It was on the tip of her tongue to add "like us" but she didn't because she still wasn't sure where they were headed.

"It's one of my favorite movies. Plus, Taye Diggs is such a hottie. Over the years I kind of thought of you whenever I saw him. Probably because of the bald head and your delectable chocolate skin."

"So I'm a hottie?" he asked, trying to give a sexy smile and pose. "Think I could walk the runway in your next fashion show? I look fine in an Elle Lauren tux, you know. I'm the right height and build." Walking, he did his best impersonation of a model strolling down the runway while she laughed uncontrollably. He stroked his goatee that was beginning to grow in and slid his hands in his pocket while pivoting. He finished off with a kneel pose while make-believing he'd flung a jacket over his shoulder. Slamming on the couch next to her, he grabbed his beer from the table.

"Can you dig it, baby?" he asked in his *The Mack* voice.

She placed a loud smooch on his cheek. "Yes, babe. You did a great job…if you were auditioning for a role to play a pimp from a movie set in the seventies."

He tossed a pillow at her and she caught it and hit him with it. Pulling her on his lap, he tickled her until she laughed so hard her side hurt.

"Aww, you got jokes, huh?" He stopped and she slid to the floor to finish laughing.

"Nah, that's how you were walking. Stick to your day job and let Tyson Beckford keep his." She stopped as her cell phone beeped. Snatching it from the table she saw that she had a text from Kirk asking if she was ready for their conference call to go over the model auditions from that day.

"This is Kirk, babe. I gotta go through these pictures with him."

"No problem. I'll get some practice in. Will that disturb you?"

"No. I usually have music on in the background when working and live music is even better, especially when you're playing." Leaning over, she kissed him on the forehead. "I'm going to the bedroom. See you in about two hours."

An hour and a half later, Elle was pleased with her decision on the variety of models for her upcoming show for the department store line, Classic Elle. She'd had some time to kill and Braxton was still practicing so she decided to shower and slip on a blue lacy nightgown. Mya had snuck it into the suitcase along with a few other essentials that Ciara probably told her to place in there, too.

Sauntering out into the great room, she found him performing an unfamiliar song that she found quite alluring and was the perfect song for the seduction she was about to bestow on him. Approaching him, she slid her hands on his shoulders and planted a tender kiss on his neck. He stopped playing and grabbed her to him, causing her to laugh out loud. Straddling his lap, she wrapped her arms around his neck and her legs encircled his waist.

"Hey, handsome."

"I knew you were there."

She titled her head. "How? I tiptoed in here, plus you were playing and humming. You were in your own musical world."

"Your scent. It's an aphrodisiac for me but you're early. I still have about thirty minutes left to play." His eyes perused over her ensemble as he ran his tongue over his bottom lip. "Not that I'm complaining about you stopping me. Damn, you're sexy."

Taking his hands from her butt, she placed them back on the keys. "Then play while I play."

Before Braxton could protest, she crashed her lips on his, twirling her tongue hard and slow as a guttural moan unleashed from his throat.

"You were saying, Maestro?" she asked through hazy eyes as his were practically closed.

"What do you want to hear?" He kissed her deep, dragging his tongue along her mouth and gently tugging her lips as his hand went the entire length of the piano.

"Whatever you feel," she replied in a sultry tone. "You're master of the keys."

He proceeded to play an unfamiliar, yet sensual, seductive tune as Elle lowered her lips back to his. The touch was gentle at first, as she relished in his warmth, sliding her tongue inside his mouth to find his eagerly responding. He returned the kiss with the same unhurried, invigorating cadence that matched what he played. Her eyes fluttered shut as she moved her hands to his face, pulling him deeper into her as their kisses and the melody he played intensified. She broke her lips away from his and placed them on his neck, teasing and taunting him as he stumbled a few times on the keys. He released a few curse words especially when she began to gyrate on the erection she could feel throbbing through the material that was in the way. Moving a hand down, she unzipped his pants and put her fingers inside the opening of his boxer shorts. Stroking her hand strongly up and down the hard length of him, she settled her lips over his but didn't kiss him as they gazed at each other intently. His amorous moans and facial expressions were causing her to tremble against him but her goal was to seduce and please him tonight.

"Damn, girl. Best idea you've ever had."

"Thank you, Maestro. Love the song."

"It's a little something I just put together," he growled as she glided her tongue back on his neck.

"I meant you."

She began to unbutton his shirt, placing kisses along his chest and scooting her body down at the same time as Braxton let out a knowing sigh of where she was headed.

Braxton had been definitely thrown off-key when Elle had entered the room. Her alluring scent had touched his nose signaling him of her presence. He had a feeling he was about to be seduced and welcomed every moment that was about to transpire. Her lacy blue nightgown with the matching cover-up did nothing to hide her exquisite body and he couldn't wait to toss both to the floor.

He grasped her tresses with one of his hands while he tried hard to continue to play with the other. However, he was losing focus as her heat-filled gaze looked up at him and her hands glided up and down his rod as his breathing became unhinged and her lips parted slightly.

"Use both hands to play, Maestro," she whispered, kneeling to the floor between his legs and returning his hand back to the piano.

Resting her hands on the bottom of his erection, she licked the tip in a circle and then all the way down. Braxton skipped a note or five and stared down at the sexy vision before him as she swallowed him into her hot wet mouth one inch at a time as far as she could. Her luscious lips surrounded him as she continued to glide up and down at a sensual tempo. At times taking as much as possible, other times just the top before sinking harder and faster each time. The purrs resonating from her were of pure raw pleasure, and he wasn't sure how much longer he could hold on as her mouth became tighter around him, the deeper she went. She squeezed his thighs firmly as he reached the back of her throat and then was drawn all the way out. She took a few short breaths before diving down once more. He intertwined both hands in her hair to guide her up and down, not that she needed it, but he needed his hands on her. He was enjoying the music that elicited from her so much more at the moment than the baby grand.

"Goodness, I love how naughty you are, Elle."

She continued to ravish him senseless and he knew he couldn't contain himself for much longer. Pulling her up to him, he set her on his lap and reached for the condom packet he spotted earlier in the pocket of her lacy cover up.

"You read my mind," she said, snatching it from him and opening it. She lifted her bottom up and rolled the condom on him and then proceeded to take her cover-up and nightgown off.

"No, you read my mind. I was ready to tear that off you."

A seductive, devilish grin formed across her face as she slid back down until he was completely engulfed in her. A fervent gasp educed from her mouth. Resting her head on his forehead, she wrapped her arms around his neck as her body began to rise up and down at a very slow pace on him. Her breathing unraveled on his mouth and her legs shook around his waist.

Grasping her hard by the hips, he raised her up and down, speeding up each time as she bounced on him deeper and harder. He held her firm in his arms as her passionate moans filled the air.

"You didn't really think you were in control, did you?" he asked gruffly against her lips.

She didn't answer. She quivered against him and whispered a few words mixed in with his name. He knew her climax was near. He hated to admit that his was as well, thanks to her lips on him some moments before. He wasn't finished reminding her that she was all his, and they were beautifully connected, heart, body and soul. Always had been. His connection with her was so powerful and right that it was scary at times. He'd tried over the years to forget about her but he couldn't. Elle was his soul mate. His one true love. No matter what, he wasn't going to ever let her go again. That had been his biggest regret and the hardest thing he'd ever done in his life.

Clutching on to his shoulders, Elle buried her head into his chest and sounded off a long gasping-for-air orgasm. He held her close as he began to meet her pace with upward thrusts as her back hit against the keys to a tune that was in beat with their lovemaking. He made a quick mental note to remember the abstract piece that she'd unintentionally created.

As Elle calmed down, she lifted her head and stared at him with hazy eyes.

Wiping her brow, he kissed her softly. "Hi there."

She smiled weakly. "Hi."

"You good, babe?"

"Mmm-hmm. You didn't climax with me," she said with disappointment.

"I'm not done. Just wanted to pay you back for driving me totally insane."

"Oh, I see. By driving me crazy? I don't mind at all. What's next, Maestro?"

"Get up for a minute."

She did as he commanded and he stood in front of her, taking off his pants and boxer shorts. "Not fair that you were the only one naked." He winked, and then turned her around to face the piano.

Nervous excitement shook through Elle as he parted her legs and placed her hands on top of the piano. She took a few short breaths to prepare herself. She was still coming down from her last orgasm and she knew this position with him would send her over the edge, it always had. His hands glided down her neck, back and stopped at her hips as she felt his erection press against her butt. She glanced over her shoulder and caught his heated stare on her and a naughty smile as he eased in with one long stroke that sent vibrations through her veins and a sound from her she didn't recognize. One of her hands slipped to the keys, shutting the cover but he quickly reopened it and whispered in her ear.

"I'm curious to see what kind of music we'll make this go-round. I might have to it put on my next CD."

Leaning over, he kissed his spot on the back of her

neck but he didn't move yet. Her abdominal muscles clenched. Even though he hadn't begun, she could feel all of him inside of her throbbing and ready to begin. In this position he'd always felt harder and bigger and she'd required a moment before he began. Slowly, he drew her by the hips to him in short yet sensual strokes over and over that sped up to longer and deeper thrusts as he dug his hands firmly into her butt.

"Goodness, Braxton," she yelled out unable to contain the fervor building inside of her.

Her orgasms began to overlap and the sounds she made were practically incoherent. She could no longer control herself as he hammered into her making her shudder so many times that her voice was hoarse from screaming his name. Elle slumped over the piano, completely exhausted and satisfied but needing more of his exhilarating passion that was sending her over the edge. His tempo never slowed as he delved into her over and over.

Encircling his arms around her waist, he held her close to him as she could feel his vibrations begin to rock through him and she sensed his end was near.

"Feel good, Elle?"

"Yes, Brax. So damn good."

"You're all mine, you hear me?" he groaned in her ear. "All of you. Heart, body and soul."

"I know, baby," she panted out. "I know."

"I'm never letting you go again. I love you. You hear me? I love you, Elle."

His thrusts by this time were out of control as he shook hard against her and roared out her name loudly in the air as she quivered against him.

His last coherent words resonated in her ear, but she couldn't answer him. Did she love him? With all her heart. But the fear of his leaving her again tugged at her, as well.

The next morning, Braxton carried her bags out to the Escalade that awaited to drive her to LaGuardia Airport for her flight to Los Angeles. She was headed to the West Coast to check on her store in Beverly Hills and meet with a celebrity client who was filming a reality show. The client had asked Elle to make an appearance and she agreed. She sat on the couch scrolling through emails on her cell phone since Braxton had instructed her to let him handle her luggage.

He strode in with a half smile on his face. "You're all set." He pulled her to him. "Goodness, I hate that you have to go. I had a great time."

"Me, too."

His facial expression changed from joyful to serious in a flash, and she had a notion where this conversation was going, if she knew him like she thought she did.

"Elle, I meant what I said last night. I love you and I'm not letting you go. *Ever.*"

Her body froze against his. She'd hoped that perhaps he'd said that in the heat of the moment, considering what he was doing at that point in time. Though, deep down, she knew that wasn't the case.

"Brax…" she sighed, hoping he'd avoid this conversation on their minivacation.

"Elle, just listen. I know I made a mistake years ago, but I know in my heart, we're meant to be. I love you and I want to marry you."

"Marry me?" She stepped away from him. "For someone who didn't want me years ago, now all of sudden you love me, and want to marry me?"

Puzzlement washed over his features as he closed the gap between them, but she stepped out of his personal space once again. "Elle… I thought… I mean our time here…"

She put her hands up to hold him back. "Just stop it! You're just going too fast for me. We agreed to take it slow and get to know each other again. That was the point of our phone conversations and coming out here but then we made love and…I don't even know if I can…" Her pulse sped up as the fear crept back in her veins.

"What?" he demanded.

"Braxton… I…" she stopped. She couldn't get the words out.

"Trust me," he said barely above a whisper. "You don't know if you can trust me."

Her heart sank as she realized he'd been hurting

as well. She went to him because she wouldn't want anyone else to comfort him but her. That had always been their bond and connection. Their motto. Placing her hand on his face, she stared up at him and she noticed the tears well in his eyes.

"I love you, too, but I'm scared, Brax. I'm admitting to you that I'm scared that you'd leave me again. I need time to process all of this. You just reentered my life all of sudden and everything is happening so fast. Just give me time. Please, baby."

He pressed his lips together and nodded his head in silence. "How much time?" he asked as if he was in physical pain.

"I don't know."

She stood on her tippy-toes to kiss him goodbye, but he yanked her to him and crushed his lips on hers hard showing no mercy of his passion and possession over her. Elle responded with a deep, enticing kiss, and a heart-wrenching moan rumbled from his throat. He entangled his fingers into her hair, exploring his tongue farther into her mouth. The desire that soared through him reciprocated in her and shook her to the core.

The ringing of her phone reminded her she had a plane to catch, and she reluctantly broke away from him and grabbed her purse from the couch.

His chest rose up and down as fire burned in his eyes. "This is not over Elle. I will fight for us. I will fight for you."

"I have to go or I'll miss my plane." She glanced at her phone to see Ciara had called and texted five times. She and Mya were probably already at the airport.

They walked out to the SUV in silence. The driver jumped out when they approached and attempted to open the back door for Elle but Braxton waved him off and did so himself.

"Call me when you get to the airport," he said, as she hopped into the backseat.

"I will."

He stared at her for a moment longer with loving eyes before shutting the door.

Elle rested her head back on the seat and closed her eyes as she tried to shut out the tears.

Chapter 11

"Why is that so hard for you to understand?" Elle yelled at the intern who was organizing the clothes and accessories for the Classic Elle Collection fashion show that evening. "All I'm asking you to do is to separate the outfits on the different racks according to the models. Each model has her own rack. I gave you the models' names, measurements and what outfits they're wearing. They will be here in less than an hour for fittings and dress rehearsal." She spun around the backstage area in confusion. "Where are the rest of the shoes in the collection? I only see ten. There's sixteen for the show."

"I… Ms. Lauren… I don't know. I…" the girl stuttered as Elle walked away to the other side of the backstage area that had been set up with comfy white couches, white roses and refreshments. Kirk and Ciara conversed at a table going over the order of the show.

"Who hired her?" Elle inquired, grabbing her coffee from the table and taking a long sip hoping it would calm down her nervous jitters.

Ciara tilted her head and stared at Elle in puzzlement. "Um…you did. You said she reminded you of yourself when we were in Paris. Young and eager yet ready to learn. Your words."

"She is nothing like me." Elle sighed and turned toward Kirk. "Are you sure everything is set up correctly?" she asked, strutting away to the main hall where the show was to take place. Ciara and Kirk followed behind.

Kirk smacked his lips and looked Elle up and down. "Honey, how many times are you going to ask me that? Everything is fine." They entered the stage area and Elle saw that the runway was indeed set up and the workers were assembling chairs while her other assistant, Cindi, placed the celebrity and other notable names on the front two rows.

Elle nodded happily, yet secretly chastised herself for being worried. Kirk always had her back and went overboard when it came to the shows and to her in general.

"Elle, sweetie," Kirk began. "I promise you this is going to be the best night of your life. All the fashion editors from the magazines will be here, the A-plus celebs, and some more fabulous people who want to see your new collection. It's not even fashion week yet! The Classic Elle fashion show will be a success and then we're going to head on over to the after-party where you can party like its 1999. I'll even have the DJ play that song. I know how much you love Prince."

"Oh, yeah. The after-party. I probably won't stay long."

Kirk coughed and glanced at Ciara. "Um…but you have to," Kirk stammered. "I mean you are Elle Lauren. People are coming to see you, doll."

"People are coming to drink, eat and be merry off my money. I'll show my face and then go back to Jersey for few days." Puzzled, she glimpsed around the room. "Um…where's Mya? She's supposed to be here. We have a million things to go over."

Kirk blurted out, "At the airport picking up your parents." However, at the same exact time Ciara answered, "At the after-party venue going over last-minute details."

Elle looked back and forth between the two with a frown.

"Why is she picking up my parents? I sent a car to pick them up and the event planner is taking care of the party arrangements. Mya didn't have anything to do with that."

Kirk glanced at Ciara again who hooked her arm

with Elle's and led her backstage to the sitting area. "Girl, I really don't know. I've been telling you for years to fire that girl."

Elle plopped on the couch and focused on the other side of the room as the models she'd selected began to enter and Kirk and a few of her stylists greeted them.

"C, you know I'm not going to fire her. She's a wonderful worker bee, but she needs to be here, not running errands that weren't even assigned to her. She must have forgotten to arrange the car for my parents."

"Elle, is everything okay with you? You seem extra jittery today. I know it's the big day but you're never like this. I'm the one always running around like a mad woman fussing at everyone and you're usually the calm, sane one trying to keep me relaxed. Of course once the ball gets rolling, I won't be, but that's mine and Kirk's job. Not yours. So what's up with my best friend? And do we need wine for this?"

Elle sighed, and shook her head. "No. More like vodka. I... I miss Braxton."

"Oh, sweetie, you've missed him since I've known you."

"No, no. Not like that. Now that he's back in my life it's different. I haven't seen him since the Hamptons. That was two weeks ago, and I told you everything that happened there. Ever since I told him I don't know if I trust him he's been quiet. I mean we talk on the phone about our day or world affairs but he hasn't said anything about *us*. It's like we're best friends again, but that's it. I think I pushed him away." She sipped down the rest of her coffee, halfway wishing it was wine.

"Well…um…maybe he's just doing as you asked him to do. You did ask him to give you time so perhaps that's what he's doing until you tell him otherwise," Ciara suggested with a sympathetic expression. "He's giving you space. He popped back into your life without warning and he knows he can't expect you to pick up where you left off over ten years ago."

"Mmm…no. I know him, Ciara. Since I was five years old. I grew up with the man, and I know how he thinks. I can't put my finger on it but I just have a strange feeling. Like I don't know. Just this weird feeling and I can't shake it. Plus, he hasn't mentioned anything else about the club here in New York he was contemplating on purchasing. He said something about a trip to Memphis for a jazz fest, and he may look around there or even Miami."

"So? What's wrong with that? You want the man to expand, right?"

"Yes, but I guess I was under the impression that he wanted to open a jazz club in New York because of me. Silly, right?" Standing, Elle walked over to the refreshment table and grabbed a bottled water.

"Ha. Sorry. I didn't mean to laugh but its business. He's not opening a club here just because you live here. That's absurd."

"I know. It's just how he said it like he would be here overseeing the renovations and…oh… I don't know. I'm just frustrated. I invited him to the fashion show, but he's in the studio with some other jazz musician producing his album in Atlanta. I guess perhaps it wouldn't work anyway. My life is here and his is in Atlanta. He could open ten jazz clubs around the United States but trust me, he's not leaving Atlanta to live anywhere else permanently."

Ciara's cell phone rang, and she looked up at Elle momentarily before sliding it in her pocket.

"You're not going to answer your phone?" Elle was rather taken aback. Ciara always answered her phone and could hold two conversations at the same time while checking her email.

Ciara shrugged. "I'll call back. It's just the hubby. He's knows I'm busy right now. Sheesh. So have you spoken to Braxton today?"

"Briefly. He called to wish me luck on the show tonight but he seemed to be in some sort of rush. I heard a bunch of people or some kind of commotion in the background and then he hung up."

"I'm sure everything will be fine. That man loves you. Today is going to be a long, busy day. Stay calm and let me worry about all the details." Ciara gave Elle a warm, comforting hug.

"Girl, go ahead and call your hubby back. I'm

going to greet the models and then call to see where Mya and my parents are."

"All right, love," Ciara said, sliding her cell phone out of her pocket and then jetting out of the room.

For the rest of the day, Elle assisted with the models practicing walking the runway in their outfits until it was time for her to return to the hotel nearby to get dressed for the show. She was still a nervous wreck and she hated that because she knew Ciara, Kirk and the rest of the crew were doing an outstanding job.

Once she returned to the venue, she headed to the red carpet and took plenty of pictures with the celebrities as well as the fashion magazine editors and thanked them for coming. She did a few short interviews about the line and what customers could expect as far as prices and sizes. Afterward, she headed backstage and into the chaotic atmosphere, typical of the mood right before a show would begin. But she loved the rush of it as the models were getting their last-minute touch-ups of hair and makeup. She went through the line and gave her final critique, removing overdone jewelry from some models or having a few girls switch out shoes or shades.

As she settled in her spot right behind the curtain, the lights went out and the upbeat music started to play. The models began to strut their stuff and Classic Elle down the catwalk to cheers and applause. She peeked out to see people smiling and nodding and her heartbeat settled down. When the last model walked out and back, Kirk nodded his head from the other side and Ciara gave Elle a hug before she strutted down the runway in a purple faux-wraparound dress, a piece from the day-and-night collection. Elle had opted not to wear the peplum jacket that came with it for fear of sweating. She was always nervous walking the runway. She waved and nodded to everyone as they stood and cheered. She stopped for a few pictures at the end of the catwalk, smiling beautifully before pivoting and returning backstage into the arms of Ciara and Kirk who were cheering and screaming like two school girls.

"We did it!" Elle jumped up and down along with them. "Thank you, Kirk and Ciara. I'm so glad this is over with."

"Almost. You have pictures with the models and the after-party," Ciara reminded.

"Yeah… I'll swing through for an hour or so but I'm tired. Aren't you tired?" She linked arms with her friends as they crashed on the couch in the sitting area where tons of flowers awaited her. She scanned them looking for one type in particular.

"Adrenaline, girl. I'm pooped but so ready to party."

"I hear you, girl."

Mya approached, with Elle's hairstylist and a makeup artist. "Elle, you need to retouch your hair and makeup for a couple more interviews and then pictures with the models. We have about ten minutes."

"Oh, yeah. I forgot." Standing, she glanced over her shoulder at the flowers as she followed behind Mya to the makeup station. "Um…are those all the flowers?" She glimpsed again. *Where are the orchids?*

"Yes. I read the cards. Most are from other designers. The usual. Shall I donate them to the children's hospital as always?"

"Um…yes. Have Cindi take them over."

For the next hour, she interviewed with the press and then hung out with the models taking selfies for their social media pages, but she couldn't concentrate through her fake smile. Braxton had always sent the white orchids without fail to every single fashion show she'd ever done. She tried to shake it off but her heart hurt and she began to feel lightheaded.

After her last interview, Elle finally headed out to the SUV and crashed in the backseat next to Ciara.

"Girl, we can finally party. I just called Kirk, he's already there. He said it's packed."

"Cool." Elle stared out the window, barely listening as she ran through her phone and started returning text messages from celebrities who had attended the show and were congratulating her on a wonderful collection. A text popped up from Braxton.

Hey, beautiful. How was the show?

It was a success. On my way to the after-party. Too bad you couldn't make it.

Me too, but I'm sure I'll see you soon, Sunshine.

That would be nice, Maestro.

"Girl, we're here." Ciara clapped as the SUV stopped and the driver along with the security guard approached Elle's back door. "You look beautiful, my friend." She blinked her long lashes fast.

"Thank you and so do you. Are you okay? You seem teary-eyed."

Ciara slapped Elle's knee as they climbed out of the Escalade. "Chile, I'm good."

"Okay. Let's go so I can show my face and then go home and crash. My bed misses me."

As Elle approached the ballroom she was amazed by all the people in attendance. She'd approved the guest list yesterday, but it seemed as if more people were there than she'd remembered. She was elated to see the tables adorned with beautiful white orchids in gold pots. Beautiful white sheers with gold ivy leaves draped the ceiling. It was breathtaking and for the first time that day, she smiled genuinely.

"You want a glass of wine, Ms. Lauren?" Mya asked.

"Sure, that would be…" She stopped as a familiar tune from the band began to play. Turning toward the stage, her heart skipped a few beats as she caught the eyes of Braxton gazing at her. He wore a delicious grin and was seated at a black baby grand piano amongst the rest of his band. The song they performed was the one he'd been practicing in the Hamptons before she'd interrupted him.

Flabbergasted, she turned to Mya and then Ciara. By that time Kirk had sashayed over with a glass of wine and handed it to her.

"You all knew he was here?"

Ciara nodded with a sly smile. "Yes, girl, I almost fainted when Braxton called and you were with me earlier today. That's why I didn't answer the phone. You know I can multitask."

"But how...?" Elle couldn't stop smiling as she made her way to her VIP section in front of the stage, never taking her eyes off Braxton as he never took his off her.

"He called your office last week and I answered because you were running around handling fittings for the show. Next thing I know we had planned for him to play tonight as a surprise for you. He even supplied all the orchids you see. I caught you roaming your eyes over the flowers earlier after the fashion show. You were wondering where your orchids were. Right here, with your man."

Elle laughed as she gazed around her area and then realized that the entire Chase crew was there along with her parents and her closet friends.

The Chase women all gave her a hug. "Oh, my. You all are here, too? What a lovely surprise."

She wanted to sit because her feet were killing her, but at the same time, she really wanted to run on the stage and give Braxton the biggest hug. She'd missed the hell out of him and was elated that he was there. As the song ended, the audience clapped and Braxton strolled down the three steps at the front of the stage and held his hand out to Elle.

"Hi, there," he said with a smile that oozed confidence.

She ran her hand through her curls that she was thankful she had refreshed before the party and placed her hand in his as he led her onto the stage. "Hi. I like your tux," she complimented, wandering her eyes over it. He was downright enticing and tempting in a tuxedo she'd designed a few years ago with him in mind. Now she just had the urge to rip it off.

"I do believe it's an Elle Lauren."

"It better be."

"You thought I'd forgotten about you?" he whispered.

"No."

He swished his lips to the side. "I know you, Elle Lauren. I know you better than anyone else in this entire ballroom."

"It's just that you've been different with me," she said with a slight pout.

"You needed time and I gave it to you."

"I appreciate that, but why am I on the stage?" she asked as he motioned for her to sit on the piano bench. "It's not time for me to speak yet. There's a program."

"You'll see," he said, sliding the microphone out of its stand.

"I am not playing 'Mary Had a Little Lamb' in front of all these people, Maestro."

"No, baby. We don't want to hear that. Just sit there and listen to me." Leaning down, he kissed her softly on the lips. "I've missed you like crazy so I better stop before I forget all these people are here." He winked, and proceeded to the middle of the stage.

Puzzled, she crossed her legs and waited with baited breathe to hear what he was going to say.

Braxton cleared his throat, glanced at her and then back at the audience. "Hello, everyone. I'm Braxton Chase." He stopped and took a deep breath. "Years ago…ten years ago, I left Elle Lauren, the woman I love, on our wedding day. I didn't even bother to show up. I was young and selfish. Immature. Scared. But it really wasn't an excuse because I hurt her. I hurt the woman I loved who had been loyal and loving to me practically all of our entire lives. That saying, you don't know what you got until it's gone? It's very true. A day hasn't gone by that I haven't thought about her, looked at her picture or said a prayer that all is well with her."

He turned slightly toward Elle as she sat in awe at his words. She couldn't believe he was actually doing this in front of all these people.

"So this evening in front of my family, Elle's parents, friends and more than likely all the social media outlets." He paused and turned toward Elle. "I want the world to know how much I love you, Elle Lauren."

Tears streamed down her cheeks as she heard a chorus of oohs and ahhs from the audience. She noticed Mya and Ciara standing at the bottom of the stage crying more than she. Braxton walked toward her and kneeled down. Her blood raced with excitement as he captured her hands in one of his and gazed at her with so much love she thought she would burst with overwhelming happiness.

"I know right now that you don't fully trust me and that's okay, babe. Because like I told you before I'm not giving up on us this time. So I'm telling you in front of everyone here and beyond, who are going to hold me accountable, especially your dad, whom I had a man-to-man chat with earlier..." Both Elle and Braxton glanced at her dad, who nodded at them with a serious expression plastered across his face. Her mother gave a smile and wink.

Elle turned the microphone off and whispered in Braxton's ear. "My father didn't show you his gun, did he?"

"Not this time," he answered seriously.

"Oh. Continue." She slid the switch back on.

"I'm not going anywhere. I love you. I know you think music is my first love but it's not. It's you. It's always been you. I think you enhanced my music because you've been my muse. My inspiration. But it doesn't compare to my love for you, Sunshine. So I'll wait for you until you're ready. Forever if I have to. In the meantime, I just closed on the club here in New York. Not only will I be overseeing the renovations, but I'm moving here to run it, as well. The one in Atlanta has a wonderful general manager and staff. So I'll be here whenever you're ready, babe."

The audience clapped and cheered as Elle glanced at them through teary eyes before placing her focus back on Braxton.

Setting both her hands on either side of his face, she rested her forehead on his. "I love you, too, and you don't have to wait any longer. I'm all yours, Braxton Chase, forever and forever."

Grinning like a Cheshire cat, he dropped the microphone and pulled her into his arms, twirling her around on the stage over and over before setting her on her heels and dip-kissing her.

Once lifting her back up, they were trampled with hugs and kisses from their family and friends. Elle was on such a high and it continued well into the night as they partied and danced. Luckily, Braxton had invited one of his piano buddies to take his place at the keys so he could spend the evening with Elle.

Later on that night, she lay in his loving embrace in her apartment in Manhattan. They'd just made love and were relaxing on the floor. That's where they ended up and neither had the strength to move.

"I still can't believe you're here," she said, running her fingers along his chest.

"I told you I wasn't giving up."

"I know and now all of social media knows, as well." She laughed, reaching up to her nightstand to grab her cell phone. She started to check some of the local gossip sites and lo and behold saw video from that evening.

He reached up to his cell phone, as well. "I have a lot of congrats and various 'he better do right by her' phrases in my mentions on Twitter." He showed her the tweets and she laughed out loud.

"Well, I guess you better do right by me this time, mister," she said in a teasing manner, tossing her cell and then his up on the bed. She slid on top of him and stared down. "But I trust you will."

He laced his fingers in her hair. "You're so beautiful and I'm so lucky to have you. I don't even know how I lived my life without you for so long. I'm just glad now I don't have to experience that anymore. It's a horrible, empty feeling without your soul mate. Your best friend. The woman you love. And you have always been all those things to me, babe."

"I concur." She rubbed her nose against his. "You're stuck with me now, Maestro. Oh, that song you were playing when I walked in and in the Hamptons, what's it called? It's so beautiful."

"Mmm…that's right, you've never heard it before. It's called Mrs. Chase."

Her forehead indented and she sat up on him. "Your mother?"

"Uh…no. You."

Taken aback, she slid off him and sat cross-legged on the floor. "I'm not Mrs. Chase."

"I wrote it years ago… I was going to play it at our wedding reception."

"Oh…wow. I see. Well, I guess you still can."

"So you'll marry me?"

"As soon as possible."

He sat up and stared at her in bewilderment. "Tomorrow?"

She laughed out loud. "Down, boy. I don't think that will be enough time for me to plan a wedding. How about a destination wedding? I hear Bermuda is lovely this time of year."

He scooped her up in his arms and placed her on his lap. "Baby, I don't care where. You just tell me when, and I'll be there in my Elle Lauren tuxedo. I promise. But first we have to go to Harry Winston's and get you a beautiful diamond engagement ring."

"I don't care. I just want to be Mrs. Braxton Chase."

"And I can't wait for you to be Mrs. Elle Chase."

Epilogue

Braxton gazed around his club in Atlanta at his family as they all gathered on the mezzanine level for the brunch following the christening of his two beautiful nieces. It was indeed a joyous occasion as Megan and Steven were elated with their daughters' special day. The twins were adorned in the breathtaking gowns that Elle had made by hand. At the thought of her, his eyes immediately settled on his wife's lovely radiant face that beamed with happiness. She winked at him as she took Layla from Megan and headed over to Sydney who was holding Madelyn for pictures.

"Hey, man."

Braxton turned to see Preston at his side, sipping a mimosa and eating a croissant sandwich.

"What's up, man? Beautiful occasion, isn't it?" Braxton asked, laying eyes on Elle once more as she took pictures with his sisters and Tiffani.

Preston nodded. "Yeah. A lot sure has happened to the Chase crew this year. Goodness. Where should I begin? Tiffani got married to someone I like this time around, Megan had two adorable girls, and you're finally an uncle and a married man. Oh, and Sydney's pregnant. Still can't believe that one." Preston shook his head with a smile. "Life sure is changing but it's a good thing. We're all very blessed."

Braxton nodded in agreement. "And married. That just leaves you, bro." He patted his cousin on the back.

Preston cut his eyes at him. "Man, don't make me curse you out in your own establishment," he said in a teasing manner. "Nah… I'm good. Not my turn yet. Shouldn't it be one of our other cousins' turns or something like that?" Preston asked with a serious expression. "Aunt Darla's children?"

Braxton chuckled at his cousin's fear of settling down with one woman. "Nope. All the Arringtons in Memphis are married. You were at their weddings, remember? You refused to catch the garter and when you did at Sean's wedding you tossed it to me."

"My point exactly, and now you're married. That thing is a curse."

"You're next, playboy."

"What about the other Chases?" Preston asked, finishing off his drink and setting his glass on a nearby table.

"I'm talking about our crew. The Atlanta crew. Besides, I've seen the way you've been checking out Blythe Ventura today." Braxton nodded his head toward her as she chatted with his mother. "You've been trying to hook up with her since the night of that paint party last year."

Preston ran his tongue over his bottom lip. "She's gorgeous, but she's not the hookup type. She's the type you bring home and whatnot." He shrugged as the gentlemen made their way to the buffet table. "Besides, she's best friends with Tiffani and I respect that."

"I hear you, man, plus, your sister would not be happy with you if you played her girl."

Preston patted Braxton on the back. "Here comes your better half now," he said, walking away as Elle approached.

"Hey, Maestro." She wrapped her arms around his waist and stared up at him with warm eyes.

"Hi, there." He leaned down for a quick smooch on her pouty pink lips. "Today was a lovely day."

"Mmm, indeed it was. Maybe we'll be having our own christening in a year or so," she said with a wide smile on her beaming face.

Raising a curious eyebrow, he tried to stifle a huge

grin but it was no use as she started to laugh as if she knew something he didn't.

Tilting his head, he eyed her carefully. "Well, I love that idea, especially the trying part."

Smiling warmly, she clutched his hand and led him to the lobby area of the second floor where they were alone.

"Oh, you want to try right now?" he asked. "Cool. We can go down to my office. Well, it's now the general manager's office, but I still have a key."

"No, silly." She punched him playfully on the upper arm. "We don't have to." Taking his hand, she placed it over her stomach. "We're having a baby, baby."

Braxton's breath locked in his throat as he caressed her stomach in a loving manner and the happy tears welled in her eyes. He kissed her forehead, her nose, her lips and then bent down and kissed her stomach as she giggled. He traveled back up to her lips and drew her close to him.

"Where? How? When? Are you sure?" He rambled off the questions as he was completely flabbergasted but happy and nervous at the same time. He didn't think they would start a family so soon but now he was over the moon with the idea of having a little baby of his own with the love of his life.

"Mmm… Let's see. Where? On our honeymoon. How? Um…didn't your parents tell you about the birds and bees? When? I'm going to say in the shower on the second day and things got really wild. And, am I sure? Yes. I realized yesterday on the plane down here that I'd missed my period. It was a week late but I didn't want to alarm you or get your hopes up until I knew for sure. I took the test this morning when you left early to meet your family at the church for the music rehearsal. I've been dying to tell you all day, but I didn't want to take away from the twins' special day." She rambled all in one breath.

He picked her up and spun her around. "Baby, you just made me the happiest man in the world, again. The first time is when you said yes and now this." He set her down and she latched on to his belt. "Babe, are you okay? I'm sorry. I shouldn't have spun you." He led her to a couch and she sat down.

"Relax, I'm fine." She patted his knee as he sat next to her. "Just a little dizzy, but not because of the pregnancy. I haven't had any morning sickness yet. I'm not that far along. I called Mya and told her to make me a doctor's appointment for when we return to New York, so you can't yell to the world yet that we're pregnant. It will be our secret for now."

"Okay, 'cause you know I was really about to go tell everyone, right?"

"Yes, I know you well. I haven't told anyone, not even my mom or Ciara. Mya thinks I'm just going for my annual."

He pulled her on his lap and kissed her forehead. Placing his hand on her stomach, he rubbed it softly. "I love my little maestro or maestra already and I love you, Elle Chase, with all my heart. I know you're going to be a great mother."

"Mmm... Thank you." She nestled her head close to his heart. "And you're going to be an awesome, loving father. I always knew you would be. I love you, Braxton."

"And I love you, Sunshine."

* * * * *

SPECIAL EXCERPT FROM

Camille Ryan secretly wrote erotic romances, and when one of her racy stories fell into the wrong hands, she had to flee her Georgia town. Now her father's health scare brings the author back home to the man she sacrificed her happiness to protect. Remington Krane never got over losing Camille. When he shows up on her doorstep, desire reignites. Camille fears the scandalous truth could ruin the business scion's mayoral bid. But it's Remi's turn to give up everything—except the woman he loves.

Read on for a sneak peek at
RETURN TO PASSION, a Harlequin Kimani Romance
debut from Carla Buchanan!

"Long time."

Camille was speechless. She'd heard him speak but was still so much in shock that nothing came out except for an embarrassing hiccup courtesy of the wine. And then she took him in. His height, strong facial features, the shaved head and slight beard, the smoothness of his caramel skin, and the very manly scent emanating from his direction made her drift closer to him.

The man was sexy and the sight of him made her libido spring to life.

Camille's mouth opened and closed until finally she took a step back and said, "Why are you here, Remi?" Her voice trembled and she got angry with herself for becoming a blubbering idiot at the mere sight of her former sweetheart.

"That should be obvious. I came here to see you, Camille."

"You wha… Why? I don't unders—"

He didn't wait for her to finish whatever it was she was going to say. He closed the distance between them and didn't hesitate to place his large, warm hands on either side of her neck using the pads of his thumbs to gently stroke her cheeks as if coaxing her to comply with his unspoken demand.

Shock, lust, confusion and longing snaked its way to every crevice of Camille's body. The overwhelming sensations made her dizzy. She was so busy trying to figure out what was going on that she had not even realized that it was already happening. His lips had found hers and he indulged in helping her remember times past.

When she started to respond with soft moans, his fingers curled into the hair at the nape of her neck. Remi pulled back, but only a fraction, leaving their lips achingly close…

Don't miss RETURN TO PASSION
by Carla Buchanan, available July 2016
wherever Harlequin® Kimani Romance™
books and ebooks are sold.

REQUEST YOUR FREE BOOKS!

2 FREE NOVELS PLUS 2 FREE GIFTS!

KIMANI™ ROMANCE

Love's ultimate destination!